Bar Down

Ashley K. Broome

Ashley K. Broome
Mandeville, LA 70448

Book Layout © 2017 BookDesignTemplates.com

Bar Down/ Ashley K. Broome. -- 1st ed.
ISBN 978-0-692-10921-2
ISBN E-Book: 978-0-692-10923-6

Other Books by Ashley K. Broome

M/M Sports Romance:
Playing the Point
Picking the Corners

Contemporary Romance:
The Beginning

This one is for everyone who cheered Scarletsptember on. If it weren't for you, I wouldn't have gotten this far.

PS I promise I'm going to update that fic.

"For me, I've learned that the best thing is to focus on the team you play for, yourself and what you need to do."

SIDNEY CROSBY

"Isabella Bishop! If you don't get out here in three seconds then you don't get to pick your outfit for the game tomorrow night." Bishop yelled from the front porch. He hadn't even had the chance to say 'one' before Bella was sliding out the door with the meanest glare that a six year old could manage while wearing a shirt that had a cat with sun glasses on it. Bishop smiled down at her as he passed over her pink backpack. "Let me fix your hair. You'll complain about it if I don't."

He made quick work of fixing the braid that had been too loose. He thought he was done until Bella reached back with a red and black bow with cartoon horses on it. Kadence had given it to her on the first day of training camp and she wouldn't leave with out it in her hair. "Can you put my bow in please?"

"It looks good, Bella Bug," He said after clipping it in her hair. "Let's go before the car line gets too long and

I'm late. I'm not getting stuck doing bag-skates this morning because your skirt was wrinkled."

"Dad," Bella whined as she trailed behind him. She waited patiently as he tossed his gear in the bed of the truck. He opened the door and helped her into the backseat and watched as she strapped herself in. She had informed him months ago that she wasn't a baby anymore and she could handle the buckles all by herself.

As he walked around to the front of the truck he spotted his neighbor standing with his daughter at the end of their driveway. He grinned seeing his number on the back of her tiny black shirt. She bounced in her Chucks and waved to him from across their yards. "Have a good day at school, Ivy. See you later, Barrett."

Ivy waved wildly at them, while her dad waved at a more sedate pace. They had the same wild, blond hair and gray eyes. He was thankful to have a neighbors like Barrett and Ivy. Bella had a friend to play with and Bishop had a friend who wasn't a hardcore hockey fan. It gave him someone to talk to about raising a daughter on his own, other than his mother. There were days he didn't understand what Bella was crying about, and it would lead to an evening full of tears and a refusal to eat dinner. Bishop didn't feel like a complete failure when Barrett admitted one morning that he had dealt with the same issue, several times over. It was nice to have Barrett next door to talk with.

As Bishop backed out of the driveway, Ivy was still bouncing on her toes and chattering away. He glanced back at Bella. She pulled a book out of her bag and began flipping through the pages. "I think Ivy loves you more than she loves Mr. Griffin."

Bishop laughed, "I'm sure she loves her dad as much as you love yours."

"She always wears Warhorses shirts to school on free dress days." Bella sighed as if that were the worst thing anyone could do. How dare they wear shirts from their favorite hockey team.

"Not all of us can be as fashionable as you are, baby." Bishop hid his grin as he eased into the car-line. He wasn't sure how fashionable kittens and puppies were but that's what made her happy.

"You're picking me up after school?" Bella asked softly. It wouldn't be long before Bishop wouldn't be able to bring Bella to and from school. He loved playing hockey, but he hated how limited his time with Bella got once the season began. They had two weeks until preseason started and then Amy, their nanny, would be the one doing all the work.

"Yes, I'll be here with bells on," Bishop said with a nod as he stopped to let Bella out. She slipped from her seat, pressed a kiss to his cheek, and then she jumped out when one of the teachers offered her a hand down. He barely caught her whispered goodbye as the door shut. She headed straight for the library instead of the playground like the rest of the kids who had arrived early. How his kid became a bookworm he didn't know, but he loved seeing her so excited about the latest adventure she was going to go on. They still hadn't made their special trip to the bookstore like they did every season. They needed to do that this weekend before the team started traveling or he would miss out.

When he parked at the practice rink, he grimaced at the clock on the dashboard. He was on time. Barely. He shouldered his bag and jogged the rest of the way in.

"You're cutting it close, Briggs," Kadence said as he pushed his hair back and out of his face. Bishop shot him a grin over his shoulder before he began to dress for skate. He had mastered the art of stripping out of his day clothes and into his gear and skates in a short amount of time. Bella was hell on his timeliness, but he had learned early on how to make sure they both ended up on time. Usually.

"If someone didn't demand their new favorite bow then maybe I would be on time," Bishop said.

Kadence threw a triumphant fist in the air. "Uncle K wins again."

"You want to hear what she said this morning?"

"I'm almost afraid to ask but I can't resist. What did she say?" Kadence asked as they both made their way through the tunnel and onto the ice at the practice rink.

Bishop answered as organized as a team for warm-up stretches, "She saw Ivy, our neighbor, wearing a Warhorse shirt on with my number on it and said, 'I think Ivy loves you more than Mr. Griffin'. That's her father by the way."

"I know who Ivy and her Daddy are. I hear about the both of them plenty." Kandence wiggled his eyebrows at the mention of Barrett Griffin.

"Oh shut up," Bishop growled out. "He's raising Ivy on his own like I'm doing with Bella. It's nice to have someone to relate to. I'm not finding that kind of conversation anywhere around here."

"Oh, I'm sure that's all you appreciate Barrett Griffin for." Kadence snorted.

"Excuse me!" Lyndsie Morrison, their Captain broke into their conversation. "Do you want to do bag-skates? Focus!"

"But, Morry," Tony drawled out. "You know we love to hear Preacher try to enlighten Bishop."

"No we don't," Archer shot across the ice. "It never works!"

"Well one day it will!" Tony yelled back. He shuffled closer to them and lowered his voice. "So what was Barrett wearing this morning?"

"Oh come on." Bishop looked towards the ceiling as if he was asking for divine guidance while everyone around him snickered. "How about we talk about hockey?"

"Okay." Trevor grinned showing off his newly missing tooth tooth. "When are you going to bring Barrett to a hockey game?"

Bishop looked towards Morry for help. There was only so much of their ribbing he could take before it started feeling less like accepting teasing and began feeling like judgment.

"All right. Up and separate. If you've got time to talk we aren't doing our jobs right," Morry shouted across the ice.

Everyone broke off into groups to run drills. Bishop wasn't going to be playing in many of the preseason games. The coaches would be trying out the rookies on various lines before making the decision to keep them or send them back down to the farm team. He and Preacher had been partnered on defense for the majority of the last two seasons. They only switched partners when one of them managed to get injured. Otherwise it was always Bishop and Preacher on a line together. They never lost sight of the puck, each other, or stopped communicating on ice. That was what made them great on ice together.

They focused on defensive coverage with the rookies. Stick on ice, stick on puck and body on body. It was repetitive and made his thighs burn with exertion. The awareness they needed to have on the ice, the constant movement of their feet and eyes to keep track of the puck left Bishop a sweaty mess, but he was feeling good. By the end he and Preacher were both bursting with energy from the left over endorphin rush from an excellent workout.

"What do you have planned for the rest of the day?" Preacher asked as he wiped the sweat from his face.

"I've got some errands to run. Then when Bella gets home from school I'm going to head to the bookstore to get her stocked up for when the season starts," Bishop answered digging through his bag for fresh clothes.

"Yeah, I like my plans better," Preacher commented. "I get to do nothing."

Bishop laughed as he headed towards the showers. "Isn't that what you always do? Nothing and workout?"

"If I didn't have to carry such a dead weight on the ice during the games I wouldn't have to work out as much as I do," Preacher joked and Bishop flipped him the bird. He wasn't dead weight on the ice or off it.

Once he was out of the shower and dressed, Bishop checked the training schedule one last time before heading out. He had a list of things to accomplish and not enough time to get everything done. Wasn't that how it always was? Groceries first. The rest could wait.

He pushed through the aisles trying to remember which foods Bella preferred this week and which ones she decided to hate. It was always hit or miss during training camp and the preseason. He felt like it was her way of testing him when she didn't want him to be at work. Hell, if he could get away with it, he'd bring her to all of his games. That wasn't what either of them needed though. She needed to go to school, make friends and have a steady routine. That's when she was happiest. That's what mattered to him. Bella and then hockey. If it ever got to the point where he had to choose being home with Bella fulltime or hockey, Bella would win every time.

How did picking out princess cereal for Bella turn him into a ball of anxiety? He shook the thoughts off as he checked his watch. If he didn't move it along Bella was going to be off the bus waiting for him on the front porch with that pinched look on her face. Or worse. She'd be at Ivy's house and he would have to apologize to Barret for being a shitty dad.

Bishop made it home and unloaded the groceries with twenty minutes to spare. The day was nice enough to wait outside for Bella on the steps of his front porch. He wasn't surprised when Barrett made his way across their yards to sit next to him. Bishop tried his best not to be too obvious as he took in the stretch of Barrett's tee-shirt over his biceps or how well his jeans fit him. "Good day?"

Barrett raised a brow as he answered with a deep drawl, "There's nothing to complain about and I got my pages done. That counts as a good day for me."

"The wonderful life of a graphic artist." Bishop nodded.

"It pays the big bucks and I get to work from home," Barrett agreed.

"What are you working on now?" Bishop asked.

"It's a sports piece," Barrett answered with a slight shrug. Bishop perked up from hearing that. Automatically his mind came up with question after question that he wanted to ask, but did his best to keep quiet as he listened to Barrett talk about the project. "It's been an eye opening experience since the author sent the storyline over. I didn't realize that there was so much that went into it. I was just researching uniforms, movement, and positions of the players, but it's a lot and I need to be as accurate as possible."

"Can you tell me what it's about or is this one of those instances that you have to keep quiet until it gets released?"

Barrett fidgeted in his seat and picked at a loose thread on his jeans. Bishop watched his cheeks flush and he opened his mouth as if to talk but stopped himself from saying anything.

"Hey," Bishop clapped Barrett on the shoulder. "Whenever you can tell me about it, tell me. Otherwise I'll wait patiently and buy it when it hits the shelves."

Barrett tilted his head with a shy smile. "Do you really buy my work after I give you signed copies of everything?"

Bishop scratched at the back of his neck and nodded.

"You have two copies of everything?" Barrett grinned but started laughing when he admitted that the children's books Barrett edited he had three copies of. Bella needed her own copy too.

"Thank you," Barrett said softly. He focused on the girls' bikes that were lying in the grass. "Really. It means a lot that you go out and buy my work, even after I give you free copies. I'm not sure my own family buys what I've published."

That comment threw Bishop for a loop. Why wouldn't his family buy every piece of art that Barrett had created? Hell, he had bought copies for some of the guys on the team he knew would be interested in reading them. If he didn't have his family's continual support he didn't know what he would do. They didn't come to every game now that he was in the pros but when they were in town, they would be in the stands with his jersey on and screaming at the top of their lungs for him.

"Well," Bishop shrugged a shoulder, "I'm sorry if this makes me sound like a dick but they suck."

Barrett huffed out a breath. "They don't understand how I could choose art as my career and not a 'real' job. I made my peace with it when I was first starting out. I've got plenty of people to make up for their lack of support."

"Good," Bishop said. He wanted to say more but the squeal of the school bus breaks stopped him. He stood up and brushed the seat of his pants off as he and Barrett walked towards the end of the driveway to gather their respective children.

Bella hopped off the bus with a paper waving back and forth in her hand. "Dad! Mrs. Thompson said I moved up to the next reading level and she gave me a list of books!"

Bishop couldn't help but be proud of Bella's accomplishment. "Well I guess it's a good thing I planned on taking you to the bookstore tonight. We can even grab a pizza on the way home. How as your day Ivy?"

She had dirt smudged on her cheek, but was smiling wide. "I beat the boys in a race at recess. It was awesome."

He held out his hand for a high five and laughed when she smacked his hand hard enough to leave a sting in its wake. They said their goodbyes before heading inside. Bella dropped her bag on the floor and as Bishop expected, asked if they could go to the bookstore now.

As they strolled through the kids section, Bishop was glad that he was able to do this for Bella and to do it as often as he could. Not all kids were able to get copies of their favorite books or had access to libraries. She always seemed to glow by the end of their bookstore visits.

Bella had only picked out two books by the time Bishop's phone rang and his evening had been ruined. His usual nanny had picked up an internship and wouldn't be able to take care of Bella this season. He couldn't be mad at her for that. It left him in a situation where he didn't have much time to find someone new but he'd need to call the agency that he had used to find Amy. He hoped that there would still be someone available since school had been in session for a few weeks.

"Dad?" Bella tugged on his shirt and shoved another book into his hands. "Can we get this one for Ivy?"

Bishop looked down at the book and couldn't help but smile. It was a book about a girl hockey player. "Sure. How about you pick out a couple more and then we can go get some dinner. I'm turning into skin and bones here."

"Sure you are," Bella mumbled as she turned around one of the shelves. She tapped her finger to the spine of the books as she mouthed the titles. "Can you find the horse one for me that was on the list?"

"For you? I guess I can do that." Bishop walked a couple sections down and found the book with in a matter of seconds. He quietly watched as Bella went through the process of picking out her books. She laid a few of them flat on the ground looked back and forth between them before putting the ones that weren't as important back on the shelf. The Others were tucked under her arm. "I'm ready."

Bishop double checked that the books were put back close to where they belonged. He only had to fix one of them. "Let me pick out a couple to bring with me when I travel and then we can go."

"But dad," Bella whined. "I'm starving!"

CHAPTER 2

Training camp yielded a team with potential. The rookies were putting their all out on the ice. Bishop hadn't gotten much ice time but tomorrow night he and Preacher would be paired together and playing the entirety of the game. It was exactly what he had been looking forward to since he started conditioning earlier that summer. There was something about the beginning of the hockey season that made his blood run hotter than usual.

He blamed the way he couldn't stop watching Barrett mowing his front yard on that excess energy. He spotted Barrett by chance. His kitchen faced the side of Barrett's house and he was washing plates from lunch when he looked up and saw him. For a minute he felt guilty for watching Barrett work, bare chested and the slight outline of his muscles shining from sweat. He dried his hands, forced himself to head for the living room and to turn on the television. Bishop needed a distraction. He checked the time and let out a breath. He ended up sprawled out on the couch scrolling through his social media feeds. He grimaced at the announcement on the neighborhood page warning parents about a horrible stomach bug that was going around. He kept his fingers crossed that Bella didn't catch it. He had barely secured a sitter for Bella during travel and game days in DC. The agency required him to disclose any illness and almost every time he had with a temporary sitter. If he lost the sitter and the he was left in a bind.

His phone chirping alerted him to head outside to wait for Bella. He shoved on a pair of shoes and grabbed his sunglasses. The bus was early. It was already pulled up to a stop at the driveway. Bishop stopped short when he spotted Bella taking slow steps off of the bus. Over the course of the day she had lost her rosy cheeks and all the energy had been zapped from her. He was used to her talking his ear off about her day as soon as her feet hit the pavement. A quiet Bella was a bad sign.

He leaned down and gathered her up in his arms, "What's going on, Bug?"

"I'm tired," Bella said into his shoulder. He waved to Barrett and Ivy as he made his way up the driveway and into the cool air of the house. He dropped Bella's backpack next to the door but kept going to the kitchen.

"Let's get a snack and something to drink and then you can take a nap. How does that sound?" He set her down at the breakfast table as he started digging through the cabinets for peanut butter crackers. He hoped to get her to eat something before she ended up sleeping the night away.

Bella sighed, "I'm not hungry."

"Eat a little something and drink your juice." Bishop set a small cup of Pedialyte down in front of her. "If you do that, then we'll get you bathed and in bed to watch some cartoons. How about that?"

"Can I watch Scooby?" Bella asked softly.

"Scooby it is," Bishop agreed. Bella ate half of what Bishop would have liked her to. At least she drank all of her drink. He tied her hair up before ushering her into the bathroom to clean up. It didn't take long before she was in bed falling asleep to the theme song.

He stayed in her room long enough to finish the episode out and turn the television off. He clicked on her night-light and padded down the hallway. If Bella was sick, this wasn't good. He was no doubt going to lose his sitter. No one wanted to take care of a sick kind on their first assignment. He dropped onto the couch and thought about who else he could ask to watch her, but he didn't want to put any of the other kids at risk to get sick because of her. He couldn't miss a game either. He let out a frustrated groan. He hated living as far away from his parents as he did. Even if it were an hour or two they'd be there in a heartbeat, but it was more like a full day's worth of travel separating them.

He would figure it out. He always did. He kept his fingers crossed that it wouldn't come to that but he had never been that lucky.

$

Bishop didn't figure it out. He kept Bella home from school with a fever and a stomach bug that had his own stomach curling in on itself in sympathy for her. He kept her hydrated and dosed up on the medicine the doctors recommended he give her. The only other thing he could do was let her rest. He had been right about losing the sitter he had lined up. No one wanted to take on a sick kid. He had started to think his only resort was to pack her up, bring her to the rink, and let her sleep in one of the medical rooms while he played.

He did have one last option that he hadn't tried yet. He could cash in on that favor Barrett owed him for keeping Ivy one weekend while he had a last minute business trip. Bishop only hoped Barrett would be okay with taking on Bella and risking Ivy getting sick.

Bishop almost didn't make the walk across the yard. He nearly turned back to pack Bella up, convinced Barrett would tell him no. He'd probably get fined and a lecture from everyone on the team but what could he do? He could knock on Barrett Griffin's door and ask for help. That's what he could do. So he knocked and waited. He was about to give up on Barrett answering the door when it swung open.

Barrett had circles under his eyes and his hair was standing in several different directions as if he had tugged his fingers through it in frustration. "Hey, if you didn't know, there's a stomach bug going around school. You should probably keep Bella home if you don't want her to catch it."

In his mind, Bishop was screaming fuck over and over again. Of course it would work out this way.

"What's up? I know you didn't get all dressed up to see me." Barrett broke through Bishop's internal cursing.

"Well, thanks for the warning but you're a little late. Bella is sick and I can't get a sitter. Believe me, I've tried. I have a game tonight and I can't pack Bella up with me. I mean, I could, but then I'd be in trouble. I'd be lucky if the trainers could keep an eye on her during the game. Everyone is going to be focused on what's happening in the rink and anything could happen to her."

Barrett held a hand up to stop Bishop from spewing anymore excuses out. "Bring her over. She can stay the night and you can come get her in the morning."

"What? Really?" Bishop was surprised that was all it took to get Barrett to take care of another sick child.

"Yeah, go and get her. If you have any medicine you want me to give her bring that too. They can be miserable together." Barrett stepped back inside his house. "The door will be unlocked. I'll add to the soup I was making for Ivy."

"Thank you," Bishop breathed out. He jogged back across the yard and didn't stop moving once he made it inside. He shoved everything he could think that Bella would need in her overnight bag before he grabbed her up off of the couch.

"Where are we going?" Bella grumbled into his shoulder.

"Mr. Barrett is going to watch you tonight while I'm at the game. I'll pick you up in the morning, baby girl," Bishop answered. He didn't have time to take Barrett's house in. He deposited Bella on the couch opposite of where Ivy was curled up and asleep. He stepped into the kitchen to find Barrett standing at the stove. He was barefoot and in sweats. He looked about as tired as the girls did. Bishop really was going to owe him for this.

He'd think of something, but right now he needed to go, otherwise he was going to be late.

He knocked his knuckles on the wall to get Barrett's attention. "Hey, I've got her settled. I have some children's Pepto in her bag, but I got her dosed up for the evening. I'll get her early so you don't have to deal with two sick kids for too long. There's a note in her bag with the rink numbers and my cell number in there. If you need anything, at all, call. I'll figure something out."

Barrett chuckled and nudged Bishop back towards the hallway. "Go. I've got this."

Bishop pressed a quick kiss to Bella's forehead before waving goodbye to Barrett and giving him one last whispered, "Thank you!"

Thanks to his built in internal parent clock, Bishop was still earlier than half of the team. He had learned a long time ago if he didn't add an extra hour in his schedule to get ready, he'd be facing more bag-skates than he could handle.

"You're looking tense," Preacher pointed out helpfully.

"Bella's sick," Bishop answered.

"Oh man, that sucks. What's wrong with her?"

"There's a stomach bug that's going around school. I couldn't find a sitter."

"So where is she?" Preacher asked looking around as if Bella was going to pop out of his duffel bag.

"Barrett was home and he's watching her for the night."

"Barrett is watching your sick kid?" Archer asked over his shoulder before going back to checking his pads.

"Ivy is sick too, so it's not like Bella is going to make her sick." Bishop tried to ignore the incredulous look Archer was sending him but he couldn't. He had to say something. "Look, I owe him big for this. Ivy's a big fan of the team. Maybe I'll get them tickets and introduce her to everyone."

"Or," Preacher drawled out with a grin, "you could make him dinner as a thank you."

"You could finally make a move!" Trevor chirped in.

"Yeah that'll go over well. Thanks for taking care of my kid who had diarrhea and was puking all night. Because you were so great, I'm going to make things really awkward between us and ruin our girls' friendship. Yeah, that's not happening. I still have to live next door to him."

Trevor scoffed, "You could afford to move."

Preacher saved Bishop the trouble and smacked Trevor on the back of the head. "Dude, don't spend your money on stupid shit. You don't need a new house every season."

"You might not," Trevor said with a shrug. "I like to change it up."

"And this is why you'll be broke by the time you're thirty." Archer rolled his eyes. "Time to gear up. If Morry sees you standing around you'll make us all regret it."

Bishop checked his phone one last time to see if Barrett sent him a text or called about Bella, but he hadn't. He took a breath and let his mind empty in order to focus on the game they would be playing against DC. He bounced on the balls of his feet and shook his hands out. He went through his pregame routine. He tapped his fingers on his bare knees to the rhythm of the goal song. It was a habit he had picked up in boarding school. It used to be he and Nate Cross who would end up tapping on each other's knees but now it was enough to center himself. If Preacher caught him, he'd hum the tune out, but it wasn't something they had to do together in order to play a good game.

He listened to the rundown of lines, key areas they needed to attack and to pass the damn puck.

For the sixty minutes that the Warhorses were on the ice, Bishop was free. All he had to worry about was protecting his team and making sure the puck ended up in the back of the net. His heart beat fast in his chest as he and Preacher skated backwards down the ice. It was second nature to catch sight of Preacher out the corner of his eye and throw his hand out in signal before they both pushed off with a burst of speed.

His blood sang after he took down Thompson Gates with his shoulder and Tony shot down the ice with the puck against his blade and his eyes locked on Samuel Roussel who was standing tall between the goal posts, waiting to take him on.

Bishop threw his hands up with a thunderous yell and crashed into Tony. That was one hell of a goal and it was just the start of their night. As each period passed by, they game became more and more physical.

He ended up using his body as a shield for his team. There were numerous cheap shots that the Eagles were trying to take. He had enough of the bullshit and planted himself right in front of Thompson Gates and watched him fall back against the ice. He skated just into Gates' line of sight, "You going to cut that shit out, now?"

"You know me, bud. I can't help myself," Gates said with a laugh as he got to his feet.

The hit must have been hard enough to knock some sense into Gates because he steered clear of the dirty hits he had been trying to get away with in the first period. It was all regulation checks. There was a reputation that he and Preacher had built up within the past two seasons. They weren't afraid to drop gloves and to put another player in their place. They had lovingly been dubbed the Bible Belt Boys. You could expect that there would be hell to pay if you messed with any in their flock.

By the end of the third period, Bishop's muscles were singing from a well-played game. On nights he didn't have Bella and the team pulled off a win like tonight, he'd head out with the rest of the guys on the team. They'd grab a couple drinks and have a good time. Instead he was anxious to get home and was half tempted to skip his cool down routine so he could leave faster. He stretched his muscles and reminded himself there was a reason he did this after every game. If he took care of his body, his body would take care of him.

Bishop woke up groggy and sore. He glanced at the clock and groaned. It was barely seven o'clock. It was too early to go collect Bella from next door. He already owed Barrett big for taking care of her, he didn't want to make matters worse by waking the Griffin household up before they were prepared to. He shuffled from his bedroom and to the kitchen. The coffee machine had been set to drip and Bishop started the process of organizing his ice packs. It was normal for him to spend the morning after a game sipping coffee with ice packs pressed against any sore spots. He grabbed his tens unit from the pantry shelf and set the electrodes at the back of his neck and his left shoulder.

He hummed with relief as the tens unit set to work. The tens unit helped him stay away from ibuprofen and the possibility of bruising easily the next time he got hit. He grabbed his mug of coffee, the ice packs and settled on the couch. The house was quiet enough that he heard the clock in the kitchen ticking. He needed to think of something to do for Barrett and Ivy that was better than his shitty cooking. Bishop knew how to bake chicken nuggets like a boss, but everything else turned out to be a sloppy mess. A mess that tasted good, but it wasn't something he would be proud to serve to Barrett. He imagined the look he'd get from Ivy and Barrett whispering to her to pretend to like it.

There was the option of bringing a gift basket of some kind over. It seemed like cop out though. They didn't work together and neither of them had been sick. He grabbed his cell phone and decided to text Nate. He had dealt with enough of Nate's relationship trouble, he could return the favor and listen to Bishop's issues. His nonexistent romance issues. Bishop was too much of a coward to make a move.

He typed out a text just in case Nate was still asleep. "What should I cook my neighbor for taking care of my sick kid?"

Nate's responded quickly. "The hottie graphic artist?"

Bishop rolled his eyes. He needed to learn how to stop talking about Barrett. He would never get away from people chirping him about Barrett. "That's the one."

"Make him your chicken parmesan. If you don't get any action, then you're on your own."

Okay, Bishop would give Nate that one. It was one of the few dishes he made that he would be proud of serving. It was a family recipe that his mom made sure he and his brother knew how to make before leaving home. Apparently they needed all the help they could get.

One problem down and moving on to the next, Bishop shifted on the couch to pull the electrodes off of his neck and shoulders before tucking it back into its case. He and Nate chatted back and forth for a while. Nate couldn't shut up about Roman, but that was normal. It was actually nice to hear about a relationship working out in someone's favor for once. He had gotten used to being the person all the guys relied on when a relationship went sour and they needed someone to listen to them. For some reason they thought he had all the answers when he was just as clueless as they were.

Nine o'clock rolled around and Bishop changed his sweats out for a pair of jeans and a tee-shirt before walking across the yard and knocking on Barrett's door. He was ready to have Bella back home. Barrett's hair was a mess when he opened the door and he looked like he hadn't been awake that long. "Hey."

The sleepy rasp of his voice sent a flare of want down Bishop's spine. "I didn't mean to wake you."

Barrett gestured for Bishop to come inside. "I've been up long enough for a cup of coffee. The girls are still passed out in the living room."

"Thank you for watching Bella for me. Perhaps I could make dinner for you once everyone is feeling better again? To say thank you," Bishop offered.

"You don't have to do that." Barrett gestured towards the coffee carafe, but Bishop shook his head no. "I'm going to make some toast for the girls and eggs for me. Do you want any?"

Bishop thought he should say no, grab Bella and her bags and get out of Barrett's hair. But instead of making an excuse, Bishop found himself saying, "Sure. Breakfast would be great."

"Okay." Barrett grabbed a couple more eggs from the fridge and started cooking. As he worked, Bishop took the time to glance around what he could see of Barrett's house. His first impression was how lived in the house appeared. Ivy's art and school work had been pinned to the refrigerator next to a picture Barrett must have drawn of them. If Ivy continued on the path she was on, she'd give her dad a run for his money with her artistic abilities. There were dirtied dishes in the sink from the night before and empty bottles of PediaLyte and cracker wrappers littering the counter.

He felt guilty that Barrett had saved his ass last night and was now cooking him breakfast. "Did you manage to get any sleep? I'm sorry, I can take Bella and leave. I should be the one making breakfast for you."

Barrett turned around with a grin, "They slept most of the night. Bella drank her drink, had a few crackers and passed out after you left. Ivy was up and down, but I stayed up working most of the night anyways. I have a couple of pages I'm working on for a graphic novel that are coming due and I'm having a hard time getting the anatomy right."

Interest piqued, Bishop raised a brow. "The anatomy?"

"It's a sports piece. I don't know how much these athletes put into their profession. I've gotten a lot of reference pictures off the Internet, but I still feel like I am missing something," Barrett explained.

"What sport?" Bishop questioned.

"Oh," Barrett scratched at the back of his neck, "I'm not supposed to be talking about it or sharing my work with anyone."

"Say no more," Bishop understood that. There had been times he had to keep quiet until the official press release had dropped. It made sense that Barrett would be expected to keep a project under wraps until it was ready for advertising and release. "But if you ever need an afternoon or a few hours to work, I'd be happy to have Ivy over to give you some quiet time."

"Be careful what you offer. I might end up knocking on your door every weekend." Barrett chuckled. It was easy to talk to Barrett when it concerned their girls. They were in the middle of discussing whether it would be better to enroll the girls in dance or gymnastics or hockey like Ivy had been begging to participate in, when Bella padded into the kitchen with her stuffed unicorn in hand. "Daddy, if Ivy plays hockey, I want to play too. She said she'd do tumbling with me."

"Oh did she?" Bishop questioned as Bella sat down in the chair next to him with a yawn. "Are you feeling any better, Bella Bug?"

"Kind of."

"Well, let's get you some toast and see how that holds over before giving anything else a try." Bishop made to stand up but Barrett beat him to it. He lightly buttered a few pieces and left the others dry before sliding a pan full of bread in the oven. By the time he pulled the toast from the oven Ivy had made her way to the kitchen table. Her bright blond hair was frizzy and in need of a brushing. She laid her head down on the table. "Do I have to go to school today?"

"No, baby. You're staying home today." Barrett lightly rubbed Ivy's shoulder.

"Good," Ivy whispered. "I'm tired. Can I go back to bed?"

"I bet you are tired. Try to finish your toast and then you can go back to bed for a little while," Barrett said. Bishop took that as his cue to pack Bella's belongings up and to head back home. Bella had barely made it to her bed before she fell back asleep. He hated seeing her this exhausted. If she was still sick tomorrow, he'd bring her to the doctor.

As he tucked her into bed, Bella mumbled out, "We should play hockey and do tumbling. Ivy wants to be like you but I want to be the goalie. Can I be a goalie, Dad?"

"You can be anything you want to be, Bug." Bishop brushed a kiss to her forehead, stealthily checking her temperature. She wasn't overly warm and he took that as a good sign. After a bit more rest and hydration, she'd be back to rights.

He was thankful for not having to head to the practice rink today. In a week or two it would be full swing travel and game play. Staring tomorrow he'd have a morning practice and then a game in the evening. Then there would be practice and travel days. He only had a few days to find a nanny or a babysitter that would be willing take care of Bella while he was working, which meant every day for over a week. He thumbed through his contacts and decided to call in one of the favors he was owed. Andy Pritchard, one of the older guys on the team, had asked him to watch his son off and on. Bishop didn't mind doing it. Sitting for some other players' kids gave Bella someone to play with and he felt like she didn't get that opportunity enough. Most of the kids were friends with each other, and that made it easier. They were a ragtag bunch of varying ages, but they all looked out for each other during family events.

Andy didn't have any suggestions for who Bishop could call but would pass the word on to his wife to help Bishop find someone for at least the season to watch Bella. In the meantime, Andy's wife was more than happy to take Bella on during the road trip.

His chest felt much lighter once he had secured childcare for Bella. He'd keep trying the nanny agency, but if he couldn't find anyone it looked like he'd be spending a lot more time with his mom. She was a last resort though. As much as he loved her, she meddled and he didn't need her poking and prodding at him trying to figure out why he hadn't been trying to date. He sent a text out to a few of the other guys on the team to see if they had anyone they trusted for childcare that might be available and crossed his fingers that he'd find someone he trusted to look after Bella. At least he had the next week covered and it was someone Bella enjoyed spending time with.

• CHAPTER 4 •

The best part of coming home from a road series, even if he was beyond exhausted, and only the chance to see Bella face to face again kept him awake. Andy smirked at how Bishop bounced on his feet as he waited for Andy to unlock the door. He could hear the kids playing and laughing inside. It would be hell to get her to calm down and go to sleep, but he'd take it.

"I don't think you ever get used to the feeling of coming home to them," Andy offered as he opened the door and gestured for Bishop to go in first. All the loud bursts of laughter and activity stopped. Bishop smiled wide when Bella spotted him. Her cheeks were flushed and her eyes were bright with excitement.

"Daddy!"

She rushed across the living room, dodging toys that were in her way. She leapt into his arms. "I missed you, Bella Bug."

"We're going home?" Bella asked.

"How about you pack your bags, help clean up this mess, and tell Mrs. Sarah thank you for everything.

Then we can head home." Bishop nudged Bella to get to work. He stood up and made his way into the kitchen where Sarah and Andy were talking with each other.

Sarah looked up with a smile, "Hey."

"I just wanted you to know that you are a Godess, Sarah Pritchard. If you ever need to get rid of Andy I'd be more than willing to take his place." Bishop gathered her in a quick hug. "Thank you for saving me this go around."

Sarah waved him off. "You know it's not a problem. You took care of Mikey enough on date nights it's about time we looked after Bella."

"Hopefully I'll have found someone to watch Bella by the next road trip and I'll avoid all the last minute panic." Bishop sighed heavily. "I'll have to trust one of the services, I guess."

Sarah moved to scribble down a name and number down on a sticky-note for him. "Here, this is who we used before I decided to stay home full time. Taryn was great with Mikey and I gave her call to let her know you'd be in touch. She's not available until a couple more weeks though. So you'll have to find someone to cover until she's available."

"If Andy wasn't standing right there I would kiss you." Bishop breathed out a sigh of relief. He could handle a few weeks of scrambling to find child care.

"No you wouldn't." Andy snorted in amusement.

"Oh come on," Bishop drawled out. "Not you too."

"Not him too, what?" Sarah asked. Her eyes flicked back and forth between the two men. Andy looked at Bishop saying it was up to him to tell Sarah what they were talking about or not.

"He's in love with his next door neighbor," Andy finally blurted out.

"Oh?" Sarah grinned.

"Every day in the locker room all he can talk about, other than Bella, is Barrett and his daughter Ivy." Andy chuckled. "He's too chicken shit to make a move."

"That's not true." Bishop shook his head. "I'm going to make him my chicken parmesan as a thank you for taking care of Bella when she was sick and we were playing DC."

"Pulling out all the stops I see." Sarah raised a brow. "But if he didn't mind taking care of a sick Bella then I think that you have a better chance than you think you do."

"Oh, don't get his hopes up," Andy groaned. "Now he's going to be even worse at practices."

"Oh," Sarah's eyes lit up. "If they like hockey, get them tickets to an afternoon game or and evening game before vacation. Let them meet the team."

"Oh no," Bishop shook his head no. "That is beginning to sound like the worst idea ever."

"No, I like this idea. This way we can see if he really is as amazing as you make him seem."

Bishop floundered to find a way to get out of this conversation as soon as he could. Thankfully Bella had impeccable timing.

"Dad! Let's go!" Bella yelled from the living room. Bishop laughed when he saw her with her backpack on, her rolling suitcase at her side and her pillow and unicorn held tight in her arms. He took that as his cue. He hugged Sarah and Andy before he hustled Bella out to his truck.

"Did you have fun?" He asked as he got everything stowed away and made sure she was buckled in tight.

"Yeah. Mrs. Sarah painted my fingernails and did my hair when the game was on. Michael didn't want to play with me because I was a girl at first, but then it was okay to play with me once he realized I could skate and ride a bike."

"Oh?" Bishop listened as Bella nattered on about everything she did at the Pritchard house to what they went over at school and how she missed riding the bus home with Ivy. "Well you'll get to ride the bus home with her tomorrow."

"Ivy told me she and her Dad were going to come over for dinner too."

"Yep," Bishop nodded. "I'll have to ask and see when they want to come over."

He took the time to look through her school folders to be sure she was keeping up with her work and doing well on her tests. Her marks were good and she hadn't missed any of her homework. He didn't expect that she would, but he always feared she'd start acting out sooner or later because he wasn't with her every day.

They made dinner together. Stir-fry chicken and vegetables. He listened to Bella chatter on about everything she had done during the week he had been gone. She was excited about the upcoming field trip that the class would be going on to the aquarium. Bishop wouldn't get to go with her but apparently Barrett was going to be chaperoning and Bella hoped she ended up in his group.

Bishop wasn't sure who was more excited, he or Bella, that Barrett and Ivy were coming over for dinner. As soon as Bella had gotten off the bus and found out from Ivy that they would have company, she ran around the house helping Bishop clean up.

"Are you making the fancy bread? It's better with the fancy bread," Bella said as she ran into the kitchen and then back out to the dining room to gather her art supplies. She had to make Mr. Griffin a card because he watched her when she was sick.

When he didn't respond fast enough to her question, Bella ran back in. "Dad?"

"Yes." Bishop nodded. "I'm going to make the fancy bread. As soon as they get here I will. We want it to be hot, right?"

"Yes." Bella nodded and went back to bringing all her supplies back into the play room.

The light on the front porch clicked on and Bella squealed with excitement. "They're here!"

It was as if Bella hadn't seen Ivy all day at school or on the ride home on the bus. He reached over Bella to pull open the door. He wasn't the only one dealing with an overly excited daughter. Ivy was practically bouncing out of her shoes.

"Hey." Bishop barely got the word out before Ivy was rushing in and grabbing Bella. He grimaced how loud the two of them were getting, but he understood it. Bella didn't get to have friends over. It was usually her going to over to other friends' houses.

"Sorry about Ivy." Barrett brushed a hand through his hair. His hands were lightly stained with ink. He even had a smudge along his the edge of his jaw. Bishop curbed the need to brush his thumb over the stubbled skin. "I swear I didn't give her sugar before walking over."

Bishop shrugged a shoulder, "Bella probably would have acted the same way if she hadn't have been sick when she stayed the night at yours. Here, let me give you the tour."

As Bishop showed him around they made small talk. He wasn't entirely sure what to talk about with Barrett outside of the elementary school. All he could come up with talking about his terrible luck at finding someone to watch Bella long term during the season.

"I can watch her if you ever need me to," Barrett offered. "I mean, there might be times I can't because I've got to focus on my work, but I don't mind watching her. I'm probably not supposed to admit this, but she helps keep Ivy occupied and I get a little more work done."

"I might have to take you up on that if you're serious about it." Bishop said as he guided Barrett into the kitchen. He grinned at the reaction the smells and sight of dinner caused. Barrett had closed his eyes and taken a deep breath of the aroma of the tomato sauces, the chicken and the garlic bread.

"If this ends up being as good as it smells, as long as you repay me in meals I'll watch Bella whenever you want. I'm not the greatest cook," Barrett admitted sheepishly.

"I'm good at certain things and healthy foods. But that's because I have to stick to a pretty strict diet during the season and if I sucked at cooking that kind of food I'd starve," Bishop explained before calling the girls in to take their seat at the table.

They dug in with gusto. Barrett gave a hum of appreciation after the first bite while the girls made a mess getting the sauce all over themselves. He was afraid things were going to become awkward if he didn't actually attempt to start a conversation about something other than the girls. "So, how's your work coming? I know you can't give any details, but you're making progress?"

"Uh," Barrett scratched at the back of his neck. "See, about that. If you were serious about needing someone to watch Bella I might have a way you could help me with my work."

"Oh?" That was not what Bishop was expecting.

"You're a professional hockey player, right?" The tips of Barrett's ears grew pink with embarrassment from having to ask the question.

"Yeah," Bishop nodded. "I played in a couple of different leagues before landing at the professional level."

"Do you think you could look at some of my drawings and give your input on them? I feel like they're missing something, so does the author. No matter how many reference pictures I look at, or game clips I watch, I'm still missing something."

"Yeah, sure. I'd love to," Bishop agreed readily. He was curious to see Barrett and his process.

"Awesome. I can go get everything now." Barrett made to stand up but Bishop reached out and stopped him.

"You don't have to go get everything now, not unless you're itching to work. I can drop by tomorrow after skate. It'll be around two, if that's okay?"

"Yeah, sure. That'll be great."

After that conversation flowed easily between them. It was easier to talk to Barrett than he thought it would have been. He was in the middle of explaining the prank Preacher was planning in order to get revenge on Trevor Liou for ruining his sock tape when Ivy heaved out a sigh. He stopped to see both Bella and Ivy with twin looks of boredom on their faces. Bella had rested her cheek on her arms, while Ivy had a hand propped up under her cheek with her eyes closed.

"Oh!" Barrett blinked and checked his watch. "We should really get going. I didn't realize we had been over here this late."

It surprised Bishop as well. They had spent a good three hours sitting and chatting over dinner. It had been a long time since he was able to talk to someone and get lost in the conversation like they had. He walked them to the door and stood on the front porch as they said their goodbyes.

When he turned to head back inside he saw Bella standing with her hands on her hips, unimpressed with him.

"What?"

"I thought I was going to have to sleep at the table tonight."

Bishop couldn't help but laugh at her. "I promise you that I would not let you sleep at the dinner table. Let's get you cleaned up and in bed."

As he tucked Bella into bed she said, "I like Mr. Griffin. He makes you laugh."

He pressed a kiss to her forehead, "I like Mr. Griffin and Ivy too. They're good friends, aren't they?"

"The best." Bella nodded.

"I love you, Bella Bug."

"Love you more." Bella rolled onto her side and Bishop turned the lights off. It would only take her a few minutes before she'd be snoring. He had a kitchen he needed to clean and an attraction to his neighbor he needed to squash.

CHAPTER 5

"How did dinner with the neighbor go?" Preacher drawled out as soon as he spotted Bishop dragging into the locker room.

Tony looked up with wide eyes. "Dinner? You didn't tell us you went on a date?"

"Who went on a date?" Liou asked as he worked on tapping his socks. He let out an aggravated growl as the tape snapped again as he unrolled it. He was still dealing with the aftermath of Preacher cutting lines in his sock tape. He hadn't quite gotten rid of all the damaged tape and refused to get a new roll. Anytime someone asked if he wanted a new roll he'd shake his head and mutter about it being bad luck to waste perfectly good tape.

"It wasn't a date." Bishop dropped to the bench. "It was a thank you dinner for watching Bella while she was sick."

"But you made date food," Preacher pointed out. "You only make pasta when you're trying to impress someone."

"That's not true." Morry snorted. "He made it for you and we all know he isn't trying to impress you any."

"No, he's trying to keep me as his defensive partner because he doesn't want to get stuck with your sucky ass for a game."

"Hey!" Archer shouted. "You talk bad about your Captain, see what happens on the ice."

"No, but seriously. How did it go?" Preacher wiggled his eyebrows.

"Oh fuck off," Bishop grumbled and he jerked the laces on his skates tight. "Don't we have hockey to play or something?"

Tony barked out a laugh, "You know when Bishop wants to get on the ice for conditioning there's something he's trying to hide from the rest of us."

"I'm not hiding anything. I just don't need any of you nosy idiots in my business." Bishop stood up and started to head out of the locker room. He would much rather do speed drills over getting grilled by his team.

He took his spot on the ice and started going through the motions of stretching and warming up before they started drills. He tried to focus on his routine before Morry would start calling out the group stretches. He managed not to be bothered by anyone under Preacher sidled up to him. "No, but all joking aside, dinner went well?"

"Yeah. It was nice to talk to him about more than the girls. He didn't leave until nine and the girls were bored out of their minds," Bishop admitted with a shy smile. "I'm supposed to stop by after skate to check out a project he's been struggling with. He's working on a graphic novel featuring hockey players and he wanted my input."

"He's going to show you his etchings?" Preacher grinned. Bishop shoved Preacher hard enough to knock him off balance and flat on the ice. He laughed the entire way down.

"You're such a dick, you know that?" Bishop shifted farther away from Preacher on the ice in order to focus on the last round of stretches. He ignored any attempt Preacher made to get his attention. He needed to focus on hockey. If he gave in and started thinking of all the possibilities that could come from he and Barrett becoming better friends, he'd get lost in the what-ifs and make more out of what was truly there.

$

He dropped his gear off just inside the house before he made his way across their yards. It was starting to feel like fall finally. He'd need to go through all of Bella's winter clothes to see what still fit and what he needed to go shopping for. He was still thinking about what all Bella would need by the time Barrett answered the door.

"Hey, thanks for coming over." Barrett stepped back and Bishop had to remind himself to follow him inside. His blond hair was tousled, his tee-shirt tight across his shoulders, but what caused Bishop's mind to go haywire was the glasses he was wearing. They were half frame and half wire. The bottom of the lenses almost brushed against his cheeks. But that wasn't what caused him to pause. It was how bright his eyes looked behind the glasses.

As soon as Barrett tugged them from his face, Bishop wanted to tell him to put them back on. "So you have to be honest and tell me what you think about what I've drawn so far. I still feel like I'm missing something and I can't figure it out."

"Sure." Bishop followed Barrett up the stairs and into his office. He stopped short at what greeted him. The windows were wide open, flooding the room with natural light. He had a table positioned at chest height covered in paper. In one corner of the room there was another desk with Barrett's laptop and connected to it was an digital drawing tablet. Taped up around the room were various pictures of some of the greatest hockey players frozen in action.

Barrett shuffled through a few pages before gesturing for Bishop to come over. Bishop was flabbergasted by what he saw. He knew that Barrett was talented. He had several copies of the comics that Barrett had worked on previously. The level of detail, how real each panel looked, put Bishop right back on the ice. He wanted to reach out and touch the snow at the edge of the skate blade in one section.

"Wow," Bishop whispered as he continued looking at everything Barrett was allowing him to see.

"You like them?" Barrett asked with his hands tucked deep in the pockets of his jeans.

"These are really good." Bishop answered. All the parts where an individual player was showcased were spot on. There were a few weak spots that any avid hockey fan would pick up on, but he could tell Barrett put a lot of time and research into this. It was when there were multiple players that Bishop understood what Barrett had mentioned. There did seem to be something missing.

He kept flipping through and slowly he started to pick up the vibe that a casual observer would pick up on. They were one dimensional and it all pointed towards the men being the stereotypical jock type. At least that was what a few of the pages gave him the impression of. He'd have a more accurate opinion if he could read the story that was meant to go along with the images.

"So?"

"There are a few things that you'll have to fix. The form in these shots." Bishop pointed them out. "What you've drawn would be a beginners mistake. Then the ankles, they have to be stiff, if that makes sense? If your skates don't fit right you get that bend and endlessly mocked by the rest of the guys on the ice."

Barrett grinned, "Are you speaking from experience?"

Bishop barked out a laugh. "Maybe when I was really young and in rec leagues, but once I was sent to boarding school, my gear was pretty much tailored to my body."

"Seriously?"

"Yeah," Bishop nodded. "The school I went to was a hockey school. Elite training, global game play, and I ended up on the Canadian Juniors team because of it. Don't get me wrong, education was just as important, but if you went there you were trying to reach the professional level. A lot of the guys I went to school with went on to play for Olympic teams and in leagues across the world."

"I did not realize people were that serious about it."

"Hockey is a way of life for a lot of people. Some of my best friends and relationships happened because of hockey." Bishop grinned as he remembered meeting Nathan Cross, the whirlwind of their initial romance and eventually the strength of their friendship.

Barrett tilted his head in thought. "I'm going to end up drawing this all over again. Aren't I?"

"No." Bishop shook his head. "These are amazing."

"But they don't show hockey how it should be shown. I'm getting the sense that you're not all meat heads only interested in fighting each other on ice for a good time with whoever was willing."

"Some guys are. No matter where you go you'll find jerks like that." Bishop shrugged a shoulder. "But hockey for me is family. But look, if you want to see what it's like, you could always stop by for a practice and then catch a game. You could get a firsthand look inside the locker room before and after."

"Really?"

"Sure. I can get you and Ivy tickets. I might even be able to swing getting some seats close to the glass. I'll have to check with media and management but I don't see why it would be a problem."

"Thank you." Barrett's voice had grown soft.

"You just have to promise to ignore what every the guys try and tell you about me. It's all lies."

Barrett smirked. "Oh really? I sense there are some secrets you're trying to keep from me, Bishop."

If only Barrett knew what Bishop was hiding from him he might not want to have anything to do with him or Bella.

"So, show me what's wrong with this form?" Barrett asked.

"I'll need my stick and some of my gear to show you better." Bishop ducked his head. When he heard what he said out loud, it sounded more suggestive than he meant it to be. Barrett checked his watch and let out a hum. "Maybe another day? It's just if Ivy comes home and sees you, she'll beg for a lesson because we're doing the rec league hockey."

"Yeah? I need to hurry up and get Bella signed up before the end of the week. She's set on being a goalie."

"Ouch, that's got to hurt. That she doesn't want to play the position you do," Barrett clarified as he reorganized the pages back to how he liked them on his desk. He started to walk Bishop back downstairs and to the front door.

"If she's willing to put in the work then I'm all for it." Bishop shrugged a shoulder. "She might find out after her first season that being a goalie isn't for her. If that's the case, we can go through all the positions on the team until she either finds something she likes or wants to try another sport."

Barrett smiled at him. "You're a good dad."

Bishop chuckled, "I don't know about that, but I try. Just give me a call before stopping by. You still have my number, right? I might have practice or it might be a travel day."

"Yeah, sure."

"I'll see about getting you those tickets and that tour."

"Thanks."

• C H A P T E R 6 •

It had been easier to get tickets for Barrett and Ivy than he thought it would have been. They had picked a day they'd have practice, have time to rest up and then head back for the game. Bella had been carted across the front lawn and left in Barrett's care while Bishop got ready for the day. Bishop knew that Barrett, Ivy and Bella had gotten to the rink before him. The missing car in the driveway clued him in but if he hadn't noticed that, then the noise the guys were making in the dressing room clued him in. He kept his head down and ignored the looks sent his way as he settled at the bench in front of his locker to get geared up. He almost managed it until he heard Bella and Ivy's squeaky voices.

Preacher perked up and he was running towards the entryway to scoop Bella up. "Bug!"

"Uncle K!" Bella started laughing as he tickled her. Ivy was standing halfway behind Barrett and Kelsey, the media intern who took them on a tour of the rink. Ivy had her Warhorses shirt on and her hair in braids with the team ribbons were tied a lot better than Bishop could ever manage with Bella's.

Bishop walked over and bent over to say hello to Ivy. "Hey there."

"Hi, Mr. Briggs," Ivy whispered. This was a new side of Ivy that he hadn't seen before. She was usually bouncing with energy and excitement. She wasn't this shy girl he saw today. He looked up at Barrett who shrugged a shoulder.

"Have you liked the tour so far?"

Ivy nodded against Barrett's leg.

"Do you want to meet one of your favorite players?" Bishop asked quietly.

"Can I?"

"You sure can." He reached out a hand and wrapped their fingers together. He had to hunch down a bit to keep a decent hold of her hand. "Who do you want to meet first, Preacher or Lyndsie?"

That's all it took to break the spell. Tony let out a groan and pretended to start crying. "I'm not your favorite?"

Ivy shook her head. "They aren't my favorite either."

Oh this was great. Both Preacher and Lyndsie looked like they had their hearts broken. Preacher had set Bella to her feet and crossed his arms over his chest. "If I'm not your favorite and the captain isn't your favorite, then who is? Who do I need to drop gloves with on the ice."

Ivy looked up at Bishop with a wide smile and let out a laugh. "Mr. Briggs is my favorite but you can't fight him. If you do then who will play defense with you?"

"Oh, Mr. Bishop is your favorite, is he?" Preacher shook his head. "I guess Bella will have to be my number one fan all by herself."

"No way!" Ivy had let go of Bishop's hand was now walking after Preacher. "Bella's favorite is Mr. Briggs too. It has to be."

"Is that true?" Preacher looked towards Bella. "Bug, I thought your Uncle K was the best?"

"You're all my favorite!" Bella laughed. She ended up grabbing Ivy's hand and taking her around the locker room. Barrett sidled up to Bishop as he watched the girls. "Ivy is absolutely loving this. Thank you for including her in the invitation."

"I wouldn't leave her out of it," Bishop answered. Morry made a motion that they needed to head out to the ice. "Right, Kelsey will get you set up in your seats to watch the practice."

"I hope you won't mind me sketching and making notes throughout." Barrett shifted back and forth on his feet.

"We're used to the attention. You do what you need to do. I'm sure Bella will keep Ivy entertained," Bishop said as he watched Sarah ushered them out of the locker room and towards the rink.

"So," Preacher drawled out, "You didn't tell us he was hot."

Andy barked out a laugh as he slipped his gloves on. "I think you might have a little competition. You Bible Belt Boys, everyone thinks you're innocent but we all know the truth. You perverted fuckers."

"Oh fuck off." Bishop rolled his eyes and grabbed his helmet. He started making his way towards the ice. He heard Bella shout his name and saw where the girls and Barrett had been set up. He waved to both of the girls before skating to his spot for warm-ups.

Tony led them through stretches. The whole time the guys were cutting up and laughing. It was easy to forget that Barrett would be watching them once they got started.

They ran one-on-one defensive drills. They were paired up and Bishop worked to get the puck away from Morry, while Preacher did the same with Tony. He shoved a shoulder hard into Morry as he tried to dig the puck away from the boards. It became a chase down the ice for the puck. He got yelled at a few times for jerky transitions. It would cost him precious time during a

game and he'd no doubt be running drills at a later practice with the defensive coaches.

As the practice wound down they lined up for shoot-
out goals. This easily turned into a line full of guys
chirping each other and trying to one-up each other. It
was one of his favorite things to be called on to do during a game. There was something about it being him
and the goalie. No one else. The rest of the arena would
turn into white noise and his vision would narrow down
into what was directly in front of him. He'd read every
muscle shift, every movement the goalie made to de-
termine how he would end up taking his shot. His chest
swelled with satisfaction at the sight of seeing the puck
hit the back of the net.

When he skated back to the end of the line he spotted
Preacher and Andy leaning over the boards chatting
with Barrett. When Andy sent Bishop a wry grin he
knew they were causing trouble. Most of the guys were
heading off the ice with their last shot and he had to be
sure they weren't doing anything that would embarrass
him beyond redemption.

"Yeah, I feel like we know you already before meeting
you today." Andy smiled wide, showing off his missing
teeth.

"Oh?" Barrett asked, slightly confused with the
change in conversation.

"Yeah." Preacher looked back and forth between Barrett and Bishop. "It's hard not to hear about you when he tells us a Bella and Ivy story. Or how you saved his a— butt when he screwed up with finding a babysitter."

Bishop was not impressed with Preacher's near slip but he did appreciate the fact that he was trying to steer them away from Bishop's crush on Barrett.

"Do you skate?" Andy asked. "We have skate nights for our families. You could bring Ivy and hang out. I bring my kids, coach brings his, and sometimes Tony brings his nieces if they're in town. It'd be fun."

Bishop nodded. "Yeah. It's great."

"It's awesome!" Bella added in. "Please come with us for skate night!"

"It really is a good time," Bishop added in. He could almost see what it would be like to have Barrett skating with him and the girls wobbling between them as they tried to find their balance.

"It sounds like it." There that smile was again. It made Bishop feel like he was the only person in the room and he could lean over the boards to steal a kiss.

"Did you manage to get some sketches or were the girls too rambunctious?" Bishop's eyes went to the empty page laying exposed for anyone to see.

"Oh," Barrett rubbed his nose and flipped through the pages quickly. Bishop saw brief flashes of some of the defensive drills. What it looked like from Barrett's point of view to have several men fighting to dig the puck out and away from the boards. He knew the detail Barrett would be able to work into those images would blow his mind.

"Wow," Bishop said softly. "These are going to be amazing."

Barrett's cheeks flushed from the praise. "Thank you."

Preacher coughed politely before elbowing Bishop. "Bishop is in desperate need of a shower. So we're going to go and then he's going to take you out for lunch before the game tonight because he's nice like that."

"If you're up for it, that is. If not, I understand. You probably have a lot to do and it's exhausting being here for the first time." Bishop tried to make excuses for Barrett before he could say said no.

"Can we?" Ivy bounced on her toes.

"As long as Mr. Briggs doesn't mind us tagging along," Barrett smiled up at Bishop. The power of the smile, it sent a thrill of excitement down his spine.

"He doesn't. I promise," Preacher said as he grabbed Bishop's collar and tugged him towards the tunnel. "He will meet you in the player's lounge as soon as he's done. Then everyone will see you tonight at the game."

Barrett laughed. "I guess you will."

"You're going to love it. Hockey is the best. You'll see!"

Bishop waited until they couldn't be seen by the girls or Barrett. He shoved Preacher hard enough that he crashed into the wall.

"Seriously?" Bishop asked with wide eyes.

"You know what that was about." Preacher rolled his eyes. "You are lucky we have a game tonight and I don't have time for this shit. You should have seen the looks he was giving you on the bench. It was like he wanted to eat your-"

A loud cough broke Preacher off. Morry gave them an unimpressed look. "Get cleaned up and don't let this distract you."

"It won't." Bishop felt his cheeks heat. The shit he was going to get if they didn't pull off a win tonight. He and Preacher trailed behind Morry into the locker room to get out of their gear.

"Don't act like you weren't going to go out and eat lunch before going home anyways. If things go to shit, you can use the game as an excuse to leave early ,and then you know where you stand," Preacher said as he hobbled into the locker room.

Bishop shook his head. Maybe he didn't want to know where he stood. He had gotten used to how things were between the two of them. What if it changed for the worst? He'd hate not having Barrett as a friend.

Then he worried about Bella. He was afraid of how Bella would react to him bringing someone else into their lives. And what would happen if they broke up? He didn't want Bella to get attached only to break her heart. He could deal with his own broken heart but he couldn't imagine seeing her hurting like that.

Despite his fear of what could happen, he still felt his heart race with the anticipation of being close to Barrett in a facsimile of a date. He rinsed the suds of soap and the sweat off his skin to rush through getting redressed. He almost wished he had worn a different pair of jeans. He wasn't expecting to do anything other than have Barrett at practice and then later at the game. His jeans were tight and wearing thin at the knees. He was sure the threads would give way and there'd be holes.

$

Barrett was bent over his sketch book working by the time Bishop made it into the players' lounge. Ivy and Bella were kept entertained by Preacher and Liou. They were peppering the girls with questions about their little league expectations. Barrett's lips were curled up in a smile as he listened to the girls go on about their gear and the team. Bishop was glad that he had been able to get Bella signed up. It would have broken her heart if he hadn't.

He glanced over Barrett's shoulder and found himself lost in the lines. It was different seeing himself drawn by somebody he knew. It surprised him to see the amount of detail Barrett had been able to draw during the practice. His admiration had been cut short when the sketch pad snapped shut.

Barrett looked embarrassed at being caught. "Hey, are you ready for lunch?"

"Beyond ready," Bishop answered, ignoring the part of him that wanted to take Barrett's notebook to keep looking at everything he had drawn today. "There's a cafe on the way home, Tommy's. They do some great sandwiches and Bella loves it."

"I know the place." Barrett nodded. "We'll meet you there and try to make it quick? They were talking about naps, unless they were trying to mess with me."

Bishop chuckled. "They weren't messing with you. We all try to catch an hour or two before the game to recharge. We get in early, warm up off the ice, then gear up and warm up on the ice and start playing."

"Oh, that sounds like a lot to do before the game," Barrett said as they started towards the parking lot with Bella and Ivy skipping a few feet ahead of them.

"It's why hockey players love their naps," Bishop explained.

Lunch was easy. The conversation flowed between them. Bella and Ivy were busy coloring on the children's menus while Bishop and Barrett talked. Barrett had a few questions he hadn't been comfortable with asking in front of the team. Bishop answered any question Barrett had. It didn't matter how off the wall his questions got, it was fun to talk about hockey with someone who had just began to find their love of the sport.

Bishop could already see it. It was a wild spark igniting in the back of Barrett's eyes. He absorbed every piece of information that was presented and he was going to turn that into art. He couldn't wait to see the project Bishop was working on when it was finished. There would be practices, team events and games under his belt to sharpen his work.

"They're different than I thought they would be," Barrett admitted as they finished up their lunch.

"How so?" Bishop asked.

"I didn't expect them to be as normal as they are."

Bishop couldn't help but burst out laughing at that. "I don't know if they're normal but we aren't all that different from everyone else."

"It's just," Barrett shrugged a shoulder, "I expected a bunch of cursing and inappropriate talk about women."

"Well," Bishop scratched at the stubble that he was in desperate need of shaving, "there is a lot of cursing, inappropriate talk about women and trash talking each other, but when kids are around they know not to talk like that."

"What about—" Barrett pressed his lips together as if he weren't sure if he should say what he was thinking or not. "I've seen articles about players getting fined for some of the remarks they had made about other people's preferences."

"Oh, you mean like who they date?" Bishop clarified. Barrett nodded and Bishop took a deep gulp from his drink. "It happens. You get caught talking like that? You run the risk of getting fined and facing repercussions on the ice. The Warhorses aren't like that though. I'm lucky being part of a team that is as accepting as they are. There are players who will never come out or they'll wait until after they retire to because of the crap they face on the ice or in the locker room. Here, I don't have to worry about it. I could go out on a date and they'd give the guy the shovel talk without fail, even on the first date. Their overly supportive nature kills me sometimes, but I know they do it out of love."

Barrett looked a bit taken aback by how open Bishop had been about his sexuality. It hadn't ever come up in their porch side conversations but it wasn't something that Bishop was going to hide. Not when Barrett had brought it up. He needed Barrett to know that the Warhorses were a good team. It didn't matter who you fell in love with as long as you played hockey to the best of your abilities.

His attraction to both men and women wasn't something he hid from Bella either. He wasn't explicit in his explanations but if he ever went out with a man on a date, she knew it was just the same as when he took a woman out on a date. Sure it's been a good bit of time since that had happened, but Bella knew. They both deserved that honesty. When she was older he hoped she understood and appreciated that.

Bishop shifted uncomfortably in his seat from the way Barrett was looking at him. He wasn't sure what was going through Barrett's mind and he hoped that it wasn't something that would ruin the friendship that they had developed. He waited to see what would come from it.

"That's—" Barrett took a deep breath, "I didn't know."

"It's not a problem, is it?" Bishop could already feel his chest tightening with anxiety.

"No, that would never be a problem." Barrett's cheeks had grown red and he started tearing his paper napkin into little pieces. "It's nice to hear that they would be there for you, no matter who you were with. It isn't something that an outsider, like me, would expect to hear a professional sports team would be as accepting as your team is."

"If we were here, ten years ago, there's no way I would have told anyone," Bishop admitted. "Yeah, the league was laying the groundwork, but I would have rather retired before even trying to have a relationship with a man."

"Oh that would be torture," Barrett added. "Only being able to catch quick looks or terrible hook-ups? That doesn't seem like much fun."

Bishop was doing his best not to read too much into what Barrett had said. Did it mean he liked men as well? Did he just mean to be supportive? Bishop was never good with reading between the lines. He needed a person to be to the point with him. He was notorious for misinterpreting the tone and the meaning of things people had said to him. But there was something about what Barrett said that left him feeling hopeful and good.

It wasn't soon after that he cleared up the check and they were out at their cars discussing getting into the arena and the process of getting back to the locker room after the game. Bishop would make sure someone would be there to help Barrett get where he needed to go. With the girls in the back seat of Barrett's SUV, Bishop waved one last time to Bella before thanking Barrett for watching her for the rest of the day.

"Appreciate this."

"It's no problem. After everything you're doing for us? Ivy is going to be on cloud nine for weeks. Bella is easy to watch, even hopped up on sugar."

Bishop let it go at that. He got into his car to head back home for his nap. He needed to turn off the thoughts about Barrett and all the what-ifs to focus on the game for the evening.

$

He'd never admit it, even to Nate, but he picked out one of the suits that showed off all the work he put into his body for tonight's game against the Monarchs. He knew what his thighs and ass looked like in the navy pants. He couldn't resist the idea of catching Barrett's attention. When he thought about the game they were going to be playing against the Monarchs, he wanted to play as hard as he could. There was a tiny part of him that wanted to impress Barrett. He knew he needed to push Barrett from his mind though.

New York wasn't an easy team to face. They didn't make careless mistakes and they would play a physical game. A game that they would have to step up and make sure they knew he and Preacher weren't going to let them get away with anything. Bishop did his usual walk through the back hallways and made his way into the dressing room. Morry and Liou were giving for their pre-game interviews. Bishop couldn't resist swatting Liou hard on his ass as he passed by with a wide grin. He laughed when Liou lost track of what he was talking about and had to get Sean to repeat the question.

"Your man is here." Preacher grinned. "Saw him and the girls walking around with Kelsey. You do know he's one hundred percent into you, right?"

"Right, I bet." Bishop rolled his eyes as got undressed.

"Sarah has been trying so hard to hit that and he hasn't even picked up on it." Preacher smirked. "I'd say if you play a damn fine game, put that suit on and offer to drive him home, it's a sure thing."

"Oh, you think so?" Bishop asked. He didn't let Preacher say what he was going to say next. Instead he continued on speaking. "Sure. Let's get the girls out of their booster seats, changed into their pajamas, convince them to brush their teeth, put them to bed and then it's on."

"Don't roll your eyes at me." Preacher shoved Bishop's shoulder. "Don't sell yourself short."

"Yeah and when it does I'll be sure to tell you all about it." Bishop laughed.

"You never know. It could happen."

Bishop left it at that. His attention shifted towards the soccer warm-ups. He could see the girls and Barrett out the corner of his eye but he shifted so he wouldn't get distracted or want to go over and talk to them. He knew it wouldn't hurt Bella's feelings that he was staying away. It was part of his routine and no one pushed him to change it because Bella was there. It was something he and Bella had spoken about, many times over, that he wasn't ignoring her while he was getting ready for or playing a game.

He laughed when Andy knocked the grate off an overhead light. He could feel Barrett and the girls watching them as they went through the ritual of the game. Every few minutes or so, one of the guys would kick the ball towards the girls to get a giggle out of them. He couldn't help the happiness that spread from his chest and across his face.

He lost track of time as they shuffled back in to the locker room to get dressed for ice warm-ups. He listened as Morry spoke to amp the team up. They made their way out on to the bright ice. It always took a few strides before his eyes adjusted and he was able to focus completely on the warm-ups. He waited until the pucks were tossed out on ice before going full speed.

The music was loud and he caught sight of some interesting signs. He loved seeing the handmade signs from the kids. He'd make sure to get Preacher to throw a puck over the glass to the boys gathered by the benches and he'd throw one to Ivy and Bella.

Warm-ups felt like they had passed by far too quickly. Before Bishop could blink they were lining up for the first face-off of the game. He pushed off to take on Theolonius. Lord, how he hated the guy. He wasn't even sure if the guy had a first name but he didn't need one with how big he was. He was six foot five, a solid wall of muscle and he only spoke in grunts and growls. He made it look like he was floating across the ice when he skated.

Icing got called and Preacher slid up next to him while the ice was being shoveled by the crew during the commercial break. He was gasping for air. "How the fuck does he do it? Like he weighs three times as much as I do. He shouldn't be able to go that fast."

"It's the momentum. It's got to be," Bishop answered.

"You should ask him." Preacher grinned as both teams set up for the face-off. His grin got even wider when he yelled across the circle to where Bishop had his stick crossed over Theolonius. "Hey Theo! Bishop has something he needs to ask you."

"The fuck I do." Bishop glanced up at Theolonius who had his brow raised but didn't bother saying anything else. Instead as soon as the puck dropped Bishop found himself sprawled on the ice and rushing to catch up with the play. The puck was in the boards and Theolonius looked like he was about to be the victor and he wasn't having that. Not tonight. He slammed into Theolonius and heard a grunt of surprise. That was all he needed to dig the puck out and pass it to Morry.

It took two periods before the Warhorses managed to get a point up on the scoreboard. They were going to fight hard in order to keep ahead of the Monarchs.

He was skating side by side with Theolonius in a race to get to the puck as it glided over the neutral ice and he heard a growl before he was knocked into the boards. He took a second to get his bearings and chased after Theolonius. This was exactly what he didn't want to happen. To have that monster flying down the ice at full speed towards Archer to tie the game up. Preacher was coming up on the right side of Theolonius and now it was down to who was going to sacrifice a few teeth for the greater good.

Bishop waited Theolonius out, hoping like hell he wouldn't take another dive to the ice. He did not volunteer as fucking tribute. He watched as Theolonius angled back, ready to take his shot before reaching out with his stick in an attempt to block the shot. He felt his teeth rattle and his stick splintered in his hands. He looked up in shock. "You fucker."

Theolonius bared his teeth and forced Bishop to defend without a stick for what felt like eternity. He really hated that man. When he was able to skate by the bench he snatched one of his backup sticks out of Pritchard's hand and kept going. They needed to play one epic game of keep away and they'd win. That's all they needed to do.

Preacher skated by and slapped a hand to the logo on his chest. It was the signal Bishop needed. They were on the same page and ready, because everyone hated guys who played like that. They followed the puck, slipped through players and stole it whenever the chance appeared.

It was exhilarating when the final goal horn blared signaling the end of the game and a win for the Warhorses. He threw his hands up in celebration before heading off to bump helmets with Archer and thanking him for doing an amazing job between the posts tonight. He had a shutout and deserved to be first star with the performance he put on. It was easy to file off of the ice after a win like this. It made him proud to know they won against the Monarchs with Bella, Ivy and Barrett in the crowd watching them play.

•   C H A P T E R   7   •

Bishop gave a few minutes of his time during the media scrum before grabbing a shower and heading back home. He was looking forward to seeing what Barrett had thought about everything. He made his way passed the guys who were lingering around before running into Barrett and the girls.

Barrett had his sketch book in hand and had somehow managed to grab a few minutes with Jason, their equipment manager. Getting a few minutes with Jason after a game was near impossible. The man was a whirlwind of energy and had lists of gear that needed to be accounted for and tasks that he needed to get done before he headed home.

"So the stitching," Barrett held his notebook open where Jason could see. "That looks right? I've got a few close ups of the uniforms and I had no idea you guys stitched the names and numbers on the jerseys."

Jason laughed. "The uniform you've got drawn looks perfect to me. And we do stitch them on. There are guys who get called up and sent back down to the AHL pretty often. Sometimes we have to put a name on a jersey on the fly. There was one time we pulled a guy from the stands to be our backup goalie. Granted, he did have experience, but that was a hell of a night. He only got sent out for thirty seconds, but it was a crazy thirty seconds."

"Okay, I have so much I need to look up on YouTube and research to keep doing."

"If you're looking for accuracy, you've got it in spades. I know any of us, especially Bishop, would be willing to help you whenever we're free." Jason reached out to shake Barrett's hand. "Let us know when whatever you're working on goes on sale. I'd love to see the finished product."

"Yeah, sure." Barrett grinned.

Jason looked over at Bishop, "Looks like your man is ready to head home."

Bishop choked on air when he heard what Jason had said. Both of the girls and Barrett looked over at the sound. Bella beamed at him from where she rested her head on the table. "Dad, that was awesome."

"Yeah, Mr. Briggs. Awesome." Ivy said around a yawn. Barrett muffled a laugh in his hand. He shut his sketch book and grabbed Ivy's hand. She made a few sluggish steps before Barrett gave up and picked her up.

"I can drive the girls home so we don't have to move their booster seats from car to car. If you're okay with that?" Barrett offered.

"Yeah, that would make it a lot easier." He was grateful that Barrett thought of it. It took careful maneuvering to get the girls buckled in without waking them up. Once they were standing upright, Bishop had to fight the urge to reach out to touch Barrett. His eyes were still wide with excitement from the game, his lips were chapped from the cold air of the rink and in the car park. He wanted to pull Barrett to him and taste his chapped lips. He could brush his thumb along the scruff on Barrett's jaw before sliding his fingers back into his hair to deepen the kiss. The way Barrett's eyes flicked down to his mouth, made Bishop think for the briefest of moments that maybe this wasn't as one sided as it seemed.

"See you back home." Barrett smiled before slipping into his car. Bishop rubbed a hand over his eyes before getting in the truck to head back. The mixture of adrenaline from winning a game and seeing Barrett so soon after was making him want to say fuck it, and to go after everything he wanted.

He didn't. He pulled up the driveway a few minutes after Barrett had. He and the girls were sitting on the porch waiting for him.

"Tonight was — I wasn't expecting it to be so, electric." Barrett scratched at the back of his neck.

Bishop laughed. "I knew you would love it. You're going to be ready for your next game by the weekend?"

"I was expecting a fight but no one delivered. I guess that means I'm going to have to make it to another game." Barrett's smile was shy and it made Bishop really want to lean in and kiss him. Instead, he settled for a quick hug.

"Dad, can we go inside? I'm tired," Bella whined.

"Yeah, we're going. Say goodnight to Ivy and Mr. Griffin." Bishop pulled his keys out of his pocket and unlocked the door.

"Goodnight, Ivy. Goodnight, Mr. Griffin," Bella repeated obediently and looking pointedly towards the door.

"Goodnight," Bishop said as he opened the door and gestured Bella inside. "If you have any questions about what you saw or anything, you know where to find me."

"I do. Thanks again." Barrett scooped Ivy up and made his way across their yards and slipped into his house quietly. Bishop rolled his eyes as he followed Bella inside, repeating his last few words in his mind. He almost wanted to kick his own ass for sounding as pathetic as he did.

•   C H A P T E R   8   •

Barrett disappeared out of sight for a couple of days. It left Bishop wondering if perhaps instead of hiding how attracted he was to Barrett, it had been written all over his face the night after the game. Or maybe that hug was too much and now Barrett didn't want to have anything to do with he and Bella now. He wasn't sure how to approach the situation because he had a game that would require him finding someone to keep Bella for a couple of nights. He wasn't sure if Barrett was still okay with watching Bella or if he was going to hope for something miraculous to happen and a babysitter would land on his front doorstep. It didn't help that Bella was having a bad week at school and didn't want to have anything to do with anyone, so he didn't even have Ivy to gauge Barrett's possible feelings.

The night before the team would be leaving for Seattle, Bishop braced himself for whatever was going to come when he knocked on Barrett's door. He was left standing outside for a couple of minutes. He could hear someone running back and forth accompanied by yelling. The door opened and Barrett rubbed at his chin. It smeared the ink smudges even more than they originally were.

"Hey." Bishop shoved his hands in his pockets. "You aren't busy are you?"

"Oh, no." Barrett stepped back to let Bishop inside. "I'm sorry for the mess. I've been working close to a deadline to get my pages in, so I locked myself inside to get everything done."

"Did you? Get everything done?" Bishop asked as he took in the house. There wasn't much of a mess. There were dishes in the sink, Ivy's school work laid out across the counter tops and her dolls lying on the floor, but it wasn't anything he hadn't seen at his own house.

"Barely," Barrett admitted. He immediately started filling the dishwasher with dirty dishes. "What's up?"

"I was just double checking that you would be okay with watching Bella for a few days? I've got a game in Seattle and another in Los Angeles before heading back." Bishop felt awkward asking.

"Oh yeah, that's fine. She and Ivy will have a blast and I don't have anything planned but a few calls. Those are all scheduled during the school day so that's not a problem."

He couldn't help the heavy sigh of relief. Barrett being able to watch Bella, it made things easier. He didn't have to worry about her needing to get used to a new sitter. If there was something at the house that she would need, he'd only have to walk across the yards to go get it. "You really are a life saver. I know I've said it before but I can't tell you how much I appreciate you doing all this for us."

"I know what it's like when you lose a sitter and are searching for a new one. It takes time. Besides, I figure I can bribe you for more hockey tickets." Barrett added with a laugh.

"That, I can do." Even if Bishop needed to buy the tickets himself, he'd be sure Barrett got in to as many games as he wanted. He might even be able to get him in a suite at some point. It was an extravagant treat, but Barrett had stepped up in a way friends normally wouldn't. That deserved something more than tickets to a game, chicken parmesan and gift baskets. "I'll get everything packed for tomorrow. I've got some cash to help pay for food and incidentals."

"I doubt she's going to demand anything different than Ivy." Barrett rolled his eyes. "You don't have to send money with her."

"Yes," Bishop insisted. "It'll be there for you to use if you need it. I'm not letting you do this all for nothing."

"Okay," Barrett held his hands up. "Whatever you want. What we don't use, I'll send back with Bella."

It would have been useless to argue the point further. Bishop had a feeling that whatever he sent with Bella would end up coming right back home with her.

"I'm going to miss hockey orientation for the girls too." Bishop groaned.

"I've got it handled. All they're going to do is meet the team, their coaches and pick up practice and game schedules. You still get to go with her to pick out her gear and be at the first practice to see if she actually gets to be a goalie or not." Barrett reassured him. "I'll send you copies of everything to look at before you get home, and I'll send Bella home with the original copies."

"I'm a shitty dad. I can't believe I'm missing all of this."

"You aren't missing anything. Honestly, it's a paperwork practice. And one of the mom's will no doubt start a group chat or calendar for the snack and drinks schedule." The way he rolled his eyes about the snack schedule made Bishop laugh. He remembered the overzealous moms and the arguments parents would get into over what was an appropriate snack and what wasn't. It carried from mite league all the way up to bantam when it became embarrassing to have your mom bring snacks. They needed their protein shakes, gosh mom.

"You haven't experience T-Ball moms." Barrett shook his head. "Never again. Unless Ivy really wants to play again, then I'll suck it up."

Bishop laughed. It was true. The things you would do for your kids, even when you would give anything to not do those things. "I think hockey will take up a lot more time than she thinks. If she gets serious about it, that's the sport she's going to focus on one hundred percent. There are all kinds of camps that she's going to beg you to go to."

"I have a feeling hockey is going to become a way of life. Isn't it?" Barrett asked.

"It will but you're going to love it just as much as she will," Bishop said.

As he made his way back across their yards he couldn't help but reflect on what playing hockey was like when he was younger. He wasn't sure how his life would have turned out if he didn't have hockey, but he was thankful for everything he learned from it. The friends and the bonds he created were life long. He still kept in touch with some of the guys he went to school with up in Quebec. They didn't end up going the hockey route like he did but they participated in rec leagues, or they had kids in leagues. Once you found hockey, it would become a way of life for you. He could only imagine what it would be like for Bella and Ivy once they got into full swing of the sport.

•   CHAPTER 9   •

"Okay," Bishop passed the last of Bella's bags over to Barrett. "So she should have everything she needs. I packed everything I could think of and if there's something I missed you have the key to the house. Feel free to go in and get whatever you need."

"I think we're going to be okay." Bishop glanced over his shoulder and towards the bags covering the kitchen table. There were grocery bags on the kitchen table full of food. Bishop couldn't stop himself after yesterday. He wanted to help as much as he could. Since Barrett made it clear that money wasn't going to be used, he figured food wouldn't be wasted.

"Right," Bishop handed over a notebook. "This has all the phone numbers you could need if something happens. Then I try to stick to a schedule to talk to her face to face every night while I'm on the road. If I'm not in a place where I can video chat with her, I'll call and talk to her. Our old nanny used to send a bunch of pictures so if she bothers you with taking and sending pictures, tell her not to. It's not that important."

"Bishop." Barrett placed his hand on his shoulder. "It's okay. You've got everything covered and I doubt Bella will be any more trouble than Ivy is."

"Sorry." Bishop rubbed the heels of his palms over his eyes. "I'm not implying that you don't know what you're doing. You do. I worry that she's going to wind up hating me by the time I get home."

Barrett laughed, "I think you're safe for a few more years. Once she hits middle school, it'll be a completely different story."

"Right." Bishop nodded. He looked down the hallway to where he could hear the girls playing.

"Go, say good-bye. I'll be in the kitchen working on putting all that food away. Just let me know when you're leaving so I can lock up behind you." Barrett padded into the kitchen to give Bishop and Bella privacy.

"Bella Bug!" Bishop called as he stepped into the playroom. She immediately stood up with her arms open for a hug. Bishop hugged her tight to his chest. "I'm going to miss you."

"I'm going to miss you too. But you promise to do your school work and be good for Mr. Griffin?"

Bella let out a sigh. "I'm always good."

"I know." Bishop pressed a kiss to her cheek. "I won't be able to call tonight because it'll be late when I get there."

"It's okay." Bella nodded.

"I have to go now. I love you." Bishop hugged her tighter for a second.

"Love you," Bella said into his shoulder before pulling away and going back to playing with Ivy. Bishop felt his heart lurch with the fact that Bella acted like it was no big deal he was leaving for a week. Barrett walked him out.

"I know I've said it a million times but, thank you."

"And like I've said a million times, I don't mind." Barrett shook Bishop's hand. "You should go before you end up being late."

Instead of drawing the situation out even more, Bishop made his way across their yards and got in his truck, ready for a day full of air plane hopping and charter buses.

$

"Who did you end up getting to watch the Bug?" Preacher asked as they sat on the charter bus waiting outside of the hotel to get their room assignments.

"Uh," Bishop lowered his voice when he answered. He tucked his phone against his leg to hide the picture on the screen. Ivy and Bella were posed over their dinner with their forks in the air and big cheesy smiles. The text accompanied the picture said, "Mr. Griffin can cook? What?!"

"Barrett is watching her for me."

Preacher choked on the water he had been drinking. The sound caught the attention of everyone sitting around them. "Did I hear that right? Barrett is watching Bella?"

Bishop ducked his head at the whoops of surprise from Tony and Andy.

"Oh does that mean you've made progress? Are you actually talking about something other than the girls?" Preacher asked.

"No, no progress." Bishop sighed. "We're neighbors who help each other out when we need it. Like we always have."

"So what are you doing for him in return?" Tony's tone was suggestive and Bishop wanted to pop him over the back of the head for saying that the way he did.

"I'm going to get them more tickets to the games. I'll probably bring them to family skate night too. Ivy will love it." Bishop answered.

"Are you ever going to do anything other than be his neighbor?" Preacher asked as they were ushered off the bus and handed a key card to their rooms.

"There's no point," Bishop said as he piled into the elevator. He shifted between Preacher and Tony trying to get more room. "He probably thinks I'm a shit dad anyways."

"Right." Preacher rolled his eyes. "You have got to give yourself more credit, man. You are a great dad. If the amount of times Kruk trusts you to watch his demons after yelling at you on the ice, then you have to realize you're a good parent. You always have been."

"Thanks, man."

"Now when we see him for the first time we'll be able to tell you if you have a chance or not. But I'm telling you, every one of us is rooting for you two. Ever since the first time you came in mooning about the new neighbor with a daughter that was Bella's age." Preacher clapped Bishop on the shoulder and made his way down the hallway to his own room.

Bishop checked his phone automatically as he set his bags down. There had been a text from Barrett saying he put the girls down for bed. He knew Bella was going to be asleep when he arrived at the hotel and they wouldn't get to talk but it still disappointed him. He sent a text to Barrett saying he arrived and they could call at any time. He'd do his best to answer and if not, he'd call back as soon as possible.

$

Practice the next morning had Bishop a sweaty mess and ready for his game day nap. They had a few more minutes with media before they were released and he was glad for it. This morning there was a picture of Bella, Ivy and Barrett all squished together waiting for the bus this morning. Bella was in the middle of a laugh, but it made him happy to see that she was doing well without him.

"Awe," Preacher drawled out as he leaned into Bishop's space. "Look at the Bug. Looks like she and Ivy are best buds"

"Yeah. They really are."

Preacher nodded sagely. "I will keep my mouth shut about her dad."

"Good." Bishop tossed his phone back on the locker shelf. "Are you ready for tonight?"

"Eh," Preacher shrugged a shoulder and bared his teeth. "If I keep my teeth I'll consider it a good night."

"Keep your head up and don't try anything stupid. You'll keep your teeth." Bishop grinned.

"Good. I paid good money for these last season and they aren't under warranty anymore." Preacher stood up. "Let's get some lunch before heading back. Then you can call your girl and check up on her like I know you're dying to do."

He trailed after Preacher. They ended up at a cafe right around the corner from the hotel. They either got a dirty look from the waiter for being a Warhorse in Seattle or for ordering as much food as they did. It was Seattle so Bishop doubted it was due to the food. They were in hockey country now and if you weren't on the home team, you weren't welcome in town. Seattle had become as bad as the Canadian teams. Those cities lived and breathed their hockey a bit too intensely.

They had almost cleared their plates when his phone started to signal a video call. Normally he'd hesitate answering a call in public like this, but when it came to Bella he forewent many necessities. He answered with a grin, "Hey!"

"Dad!" Bella was walking around the living room of Barrett's house. He spotted some of Bella's belongings on the floor. He'd have to talk to Barrett later about Bella's responsibility to clean up her own messes. "Guess what we did today in class?"

"What did you do?"

"They let us paint." Bella rushed towards the kitchen and flipped the phone for Bishop to see her work. She had drawn what looked like the two of them ice-skating. The blades on their skates were extremely long, and he might have only had one leg but he got the gist of what she was trying to portray. "That's me and that's you."

"It looks great. What else did you do today?"

"Just school," Bella answered. "It was boring."

"Oh, just school. I see." Bishop grinned. "Have you been good for Mr. Griffin? Are you picking up after yourself and listening to what he tells you to do?"

"She's been great!" Barrett yelled from out of the visual range of the camera. After a few seconds he appeared with those glasses just over Bella's shoulder. "We're about to clean up and have some dinner."

"Awesome. She's been good though?" Bishop asked and Bella handed the phone over before running off causing Barrett to laugh. He adjusted his glasses before answering. "It's only been a day. I think we're going to be okay though. She and Ivy are keeping each other entertained."

"Sorry. I don't want her to be any trouble or for her to interfere with your work."

"I heard we're going to see you at some games!" Preacher broke into the conversation as he leaned into frame.

"That's what he was telling us." Barrett grinned.

Preach smirked at Bishop as he patted him on the shoulder. "Good! He needs someone besides his Mom to watch him play. Well, I'm going to head back to the hotel. It was good talking to you."

"You too," Barrett said. "Let me go get Bella back over here to say good bye to you."

"Hey, thank you. For everything. Seriously."

Barrett gave Bishop a soft smile. There was something about the gentle curl of his lips that made it feel like there were butterflies fluttering in Bishop's stomach. He pushed that feeling to the back of his mind as he and Bella had said their goodbyes and ended the call. He took care of the bill that Preacher had graciously left him with and made his way back to the hotel.

$

The game against Seattle was rough. There wasn't any better way to put it. The Warhorses weren't playing their best and it showed in the score, 5-1. It burned to lose like that. Having to pile up on a bus, hop on a plane and arrive in the next city didn't help soothe their frustration. The only bright spot were the pictures Barrett sent him. Ivy wore her jersey to school and Bella wore her Warhorses dress. They both had their hair braided and decorated with bows. Due to the time difference, hockey orientation for the girls and the game starting, Bishop didn't get a chance to speak with Bella. It was nice to get the pictures from Barrett of the girls meeting their coaches and their schedules.

"Bug looks like she's having fun with Mr. Griffin," Preacher commented over Bishop's shoulder. His brow arced up as he hummed under his breath.

Bishop shoved his phone in his pocket. "Yeah, she does look like she's doing well."

Preacher patted Bishop on the shoulder, "You'll get to talk to her in the morning. Tomorrow it'll be Saturday and she doesn't have school. Time zones won't keep you from talking to her."

"I'd get up early if I had to." Bishop admitted with a yawn. He rubbed at his eyes. "I'm ready to pass out for the night."

"Agreed. Time to end this nightmare of a fucking day and start over against Los Angeles."

"Fucking right, bud," Bishop mumbled. "Fucking right."

• CHAPTER 10 •

The wakeup call came too soon in Los Angeles. Bishop forced himself out of bed and into the shower. What he would give for today's skate to be optional. Instead he showered, dressed and blended his first protein shake of the day. He wasn't the only guy feeling the pull of exhaustion from a mixture of game play and travel. Hopefully they wouldn't face complete hell from coach for their shit play against Seattle. They had a team dinner and then a game the next day. If it wasn't required for him to participate, he'd skip dinner and sleep.

Everyone was quiet on the bus ride to the rink. Morry had grabbed a couple of the rookies and were talking to them at the front of the bus on the ride over. Bishop normally would have tried to listen in. Even though he had been a Warhorse and played with Morry for a few seasons, there was always some bit of information that he could use to fine tune his own game play. Today he was distracted by the texts that Barrett had been sending him. There were pictures of the girls out at a park and a steady stream of texts back and forth.

"I hate drawing. Why do I do this for a living again? Oh that's right. I don't want to be broke."

Bishop rolled his eyes. He had heard that plenty of times from his brother, Brad, who hated teaching every year around the holidays. He shot back with, *"You love your job. Stop being lazy and work."*

"I am not lazy. I am taking a break full of hate and frustration."

It sure looked like a break full of hate in frustration. The girls were hanging out eating ice cream and he was spending the day in the sun. *"Sure looks like a bad day. That ice cream just ruins it all."*

"It does! It ruins everything."

"What else are you up to this weekend?" Bishop texted back to change the subject.

"Hockey orientation this evening. Figure I'll bring the girls for pizza. No plans other than that."

"Send me pics of the paper work. I need to get her ready for goalie tryouts when I get home."

"Just remember, it's under eights league. She isn't trying out for a spot with the Warhorses. This is supposed to be F-U-N!"

Bishop rolled his eyes. He knew it was supposed to be fun. He wasn't going to push hockey on Bella. He wasn't that kind of dad. He'd encourage her to keep trying sports out until she found something she liked, but he did hope that she would stick with hockey. *"It will be fun. I'll even bring princess snacks if that's what she wants."*

"LOL I can only imagine you passing out pink princess snacks. 'Now girls, one at a time.'"

Bishop barked out a laugh. A lot of the guys turned around to give him curious looks. Preacher raised a brow waiting for some kind of explanation. Bishop shrugged a shoulder and planned on ignoring the questioning looks until Preacher grabbed the phone out of his hands. He read the texts quickly before pinning Bishop with a look. "Since when do you two flirt?"

"What?" Bishop sputtered.

"Uh oh, is Briggs finally making a move on neighbor boy?" Liou whooped. "It's about time!"

Bishop could feel his cheeks burning from all the attention. He tried to hide his face from Preacher who snapped a picture of him and sent it to Barrett. He snatched his phone back.

"Seriously? If you fuck this up, we are no longer defense mates. You can go work with Liou and hope he knows how to pick up your slack."

"Hey!" Liou protested and Preacher's eyes widened. Oh, he stepped right into that one. He had to shove his phone into his back pocket so Preacher wouldn't be able to grab it again. "You don't get to do that."

"Oh, Bishop pulled the dad voice out on you. You better sit down or he's going to turn this car around."

Andy choked on the coffee he was trying to drink. Once he had cleared his throat he turned to look back at them. "You know, you really did pull the dad voice out. You might want to tone that down, bud."

"You can all fuck off." Bishop crossed his arms over his chest. He ignored the loud laughter. They couldn't get to the practice rink fast enough.

$

They were at dinner when Bella called. Most of the guys were busy talking to each other and shoveling food in their mouths like they hadn't eaten all day. Instead of waiting to call her back, he excused himself from the table and stepped outside the restaurant to talk with her.

"Hey, Bug."

"Dad! I get to try out for goalie!" Bella yelled into his ear.

"I know. Mr. Griffin sent me your schedule. I'll get to be there to see you try out and then to get your gear," Bishop answered. He liked the fact that the coaches had gear for them to try out as goalie and once they decided who which two players got the position, they'd get their own gear at that point.

"Ivy doesn't want to be a goalie. She wants to play defense." Bella made a vomit sound. "You should adopt her or something."

"I think her Dad might have a problem with that." Bishop chuckled. "How's school been going?"

"We had a spelling test Friday. Mr. Griffin made us write our words and spell them out loud, like three times the night before."

"Well I bet it made your test easier, didn't it?"

"No," Bella said just to be cross.

"What are you guys doing this weekend?" Bishop asked.

"Hockey!" Bella answered with a shriek. "I have to go get Ivy to get her to shoot pucks at me."

The phone dropped and Bishop hoped Barrett had them geared up well enough that injuries would be minimal.

"I'll have you know that they aren't actually practicing. They won't until they get their helmets and pads and an actual puck," Barrett said into the phone. "They're shadow hockey playing? If that makes sense."

Bishop laughed. "Yeah. I get what you mean. She isn't being too much trouble is she?"

Barrett sighed loudly. "Like I've told you before, she isn't any trouble."

"Pull the other. I don't believe that for a minute." Bishop rolled his eyes. He heard the horror stories of what Bella was like when he was away. She could be a handful in the worst way possible.

"She didn't want to practice her words for the spelling test and got a little picky about her lunch for school, but we worked it out," Barrett admitted. They were quite for a moment before Barrett broke the silence. "Sorry about the game in Seattle. That looked rough."

"You watched?" Bishop was surprised.

"Of course I did. I had to see how you played. The hit you took in the second was ridiculous. You got up like you didn't get mowed down by whoever the fuck that was."

"Gunner." Bishop shook his head. That guy always played with a chip on his shoulder. "It wasn't as bad as it looked."

"Right. I bet you aren't bruised under those pads now."

"I didn't say it didn't hurt." Bishop chuckled.

"Well take care of yourself better," Barrett scolded him. "I'll let you go. Bella said you were eating when she ran by and dropped the phone on my desk."

"Yeah but I'd rather be out here talking to you than back in there. They're being dicks."

Barrett laughed, "I'm not all that interesting."

"You are," Bishop said. "I better go back in though before they send someone out to look for me. Tell Bug I love her and will be home in a couple of days. I'll try to get a point for Ivy."

"If I tell her that you better make it happen," Barrett warned him. "Go eat, have a goodnight."

"You too." Bishop ended the call and made his way back in. Almost everyone was done eating. He'd have to take the rest of his dinner to-go. He was ready to head back to the hotel and get some sleep. He'd be skipping the poker game Liou set up earlier. He had game tape he could watch to prepare for tomorrow's game.

Bishop had barely managed to knock on the door when Barrett opened it with a bright smile. "You're back earlier than we thought you would be."

"There weren't any travel delays. I figured it wasn't too late to come pick up Bella tonight instead of in the morning," Bishop answered. His suit was rumpled from travel and it felt like he smelled like stale air and travel food. He wasn't prepared for the hug he got from Barrett. It had been so unexpected, he almost didn't return it. When he did, he tried his best not to let himself linger as long he wanted to. It felt good to come home to someone who wanted to touch and see him again. It sent a thrill down his spine that there might be a tiny chance that Barrett could be experiencing similar feelings that Bishop was.

"Sorry it's so late."

"It's barely ten o'clock. I'm sure Bella won't mind being woken up as long as it is you being the person that wakes her up." Barrett stepped back to let him inside the house and started towards the girls' room. "I think you may end up fighting Ivy to get Bella back though. They are hockey sisters now. Or blood sisters? I'm not entirely sure. They decided they needed to be sisters while Bella's been here."

"Did they?" Bishop chuckled.

"Amongst other things. She has lots of stories to tell you about. I hope you weren't intending to get any rest tonight," Barrett said as he opened the door. Both of the girls were half asleep, but as soon as Bella spotted her dad in the glow of the nightlight, she shot out of bed and into his arms.

"Dad! You're back."

Bishop held Bella tight to his chest. He pressed his nose to her hair and pressed a kiss to her cheek. "I missed you, Bug."

"I missed you, too." Bella yawned into his shoulder.

"Are you ready to go home?" He asked her.

"We have hockey tomorrow. Since you're home you can bring me."

"Yes you do. I get to bring you and we get to see if you can be goalie or not." Bishop waved to a sleepy Ivy as he followed Barrett out of the room and into the hallway.

"I didn't have any of her stuff packed, but I can get it all together if you don't mind waiting a few minutes?" Barrett offered.

"No, don't worry about it. I can stop by in the morning or after lunch and get it all. I don't want to bother Ivy any more than we have."

"It's no bother." Barrett tucked his hands in the back pockets of his jeans. "Here, let me get the door. Get some rest. You look dead on your feet."

"Thank you." Bishop nodded. "I know I've said it a million times and will probably say it a million more, but thank you."

"I told you it's no trouble." Barrett leaned against the door frame.

"Goodnight, Barrett," Bishop said softly as he started towards his house. It took a few minutes to get Bella settled in her bed and back to sleep. He stepped into the shower with the intention of a quick scrub and getting in to bed. Once he was there, his body had other things in mind. He let his hand drift down to stroke himself. The first sparks of arousal flickered along his spine. He braced a forearm against the shower wall and let the water slide down his skin. The heat of the water, the memory of Barrett's arms around him, had him quickening his pace. He wanted to know what it felt like to have Barrett's hands on him. It had been a while since he had last gotten off. It wasn't surprising that that was all it took to tip him over. He stayed standing in the shower, letting the steam soothe him. He crawled into bed wishing he wasn't going to be alone again.

Bishop camped out on the couch until Bella dragged herself down the stairs and demanded breakfast. Cold, sugary cereal was an excellent choice for the both of them. He'd make a protein shake before getting them both dressed and over to Barrett's to pick up Bella's belongings. He had stopped at the ATM on the way back and would leave some money, even if Barrett said he didn't want it. He wasn't going to let Barrett take care of his kid for free, no matter how many favors they might end up exchanging.

He knew that it would only be a few more times that he'd need to rely on Barrett to help out until he got a permanent sitter for Bella. It was close to lunch by the time he got Bella into regular clothes and they made the trek across the yards. He knocked on the door and Ivy yanked it open still clad in her pajamas, with a screech, "Bella! You're back!"

Bishop watched the two girls skirt around Barrett and into the play room. "Hey, I hope I'm not too early coming to pick her stuff up."

"No, we've just been lazy all morning." Barrett said as he padded into the living room. He had set up shop on the couch. He had a huge clip board and was working on inking different panels. Bishop did his best not to be too nosy, but he couldn't help himself. He wanted to see the progress Barrett had made since coming to practice and the game. He must have been caught trying to look when Barrett sat down on the couch and gestured for Bishop to sit next to him. He angled the clipboard to make it easier for Bishop to see.

He pointed to the top left panel, "It reads left to right and then down."

It was a game scene. There was a wide shot of the face-off at center ice. Followed by drawn skates, but Bishop could feel the burst of speed that Barrett attempted to draw in. It worked. He liked the close up view of the stick and puck work followed by a player or group of players. He didn't need the words to read the story. What Barrett had drawn was all he needed to understand what was going on.

"I know I've said it before, but this merits being said again. You are extremely talented," Bishop commented as he looked up from the page. He was startled to see Barrett was looking directly at him.

"Thanks but with some of the stuff you guys pull on the ice, I'd argue that there's more talent there than what I have." Barrett brushed the compliment off, but Bishop wasn't going to let him get away with it. "That's years of training and communication. But what you've got, this is another level of talent."

"If you say so." Barrett shrugged a shoulder.

"I do." Bishop smirked and ran his fingers through his hair. "Let me grab Bella and her belongings so we can be out of your hair for a couple of days. I don't want you to get sick of us too soon," Bishop joked.

"I wouldn't ever get tired of you." His ears tinged red with the admission, as if he hadn't planned on saying those words. They were the ones that escaped his lips. "Uh, so Bella's stuff. Most of it's in Ivy's room."

Bishop didn't let his mind linger over those words for long. He was likely to drive himself crazy if he did. He focused on packing as much of Bella's stuff in her bag and juggling the rest in his arms while Bella marched out of the Griffin house in a huff. She wanted to go grocery shopping just as much as Bishop did. At least this way he'd keep his mind off of Barrett.

CHAPTER 12

"I think Barrett might have been flirting with me," Bishop whispered to Preacher as they were gearing up for practice.

"What?" Preacher's voice raised with surprise. "Seriously?"

"Keep it down." Bishop looked around the locker room to be sure no one had heard Preacher or had decided to be nosy. "It's just something he said and the way he's been acting recently. It may just be me making shit up because I like him, but I think I'm not the only one with feelings."

"What happened? I mean I know you guys talk at the bus stop in the mornings and he's been watching Bella but you've been pretty closed lipped about the whole thing."

Bishop debated on whether or not he should share everything with Preacher or if he should just wait to call Nate and ask his advice. He knew Preacher was the one person here who would bluntly tell him if he was making things up. He went through everything he could think of to give Preacher a better picture of why he would think Barrett might return his feelings.

Preacher mulled everything over with his lips pressed together and looking up at the ceiling as if he could find all the answers up there. "I think that you might be on to something and you should finally make a move like we have been telling you for months."

Morry stopped in front of them with a questioning look. "What have we been telling Bishop for months?

"Oh," Preacher said nonchalantly, "nothing really. Just the fact that he should ask Barrett out."

"We're back on this?" Morry let out a groan. "Just ask him out so everyone will stop bugging you about it. It would save us all a lot of trouble."

Bishop let out sigh. It would get the rest of the team to stop badgering him about it so often. The worst that could happen would be it becoming awkward between them for a little while. Okay, things could get awkward between them for all the girls' hockey games, every morning at the bus stop, and every time they passed each other going in and out of the neighborhood. He could hear Nate's voice in the back of his head saying, 'man up or shut up'.

He made his way to the practice rink and made a decision. The next time he thought he saw any inkling of a possibility, he would take the chance to let Barrett know how he felt.

$

Bella's excitement for her first official practice as a goalie was too much for her tiny body to contain. She was bouncing in her seat in the truck with enough force to shake the truck when they were stopped at a red light.

"Bella, you have got to calm down. You want to have some energy for practice, don't you?"

"Yes." Bella nodded. She stopped bouncing in her seat but started humming loudly.

"Bug," Bishop breathed out. "Leave it on the ice. It's going to be a long practice. You have to get in your gear, to the ice, do the drills, and then get out of your gear before we can come home."

"I can't help it," Bella drawled out.

"Yes, you can." Bishop rubbed at his eyes. He pulled into the parking lot and spotted Barrett's car. He parked a spot over from there. He grabbed Bella's gear back to drag it from the car but handed it over as soon as Bella was on her feet. The look she gave him made him want to laugh. "You're the goalie. You have to carry your gear."

"But that bag is huge!" Bella protested.

"Yeah, it is. This is part of being a hockey player. You have to take care of your gear and lug it around. You win a game? I'll carry it out after, but you have to carry it in."

"This isn't fair," Bella grumbled as she grabbed her bag and started the slow trek into the rink. Bishop couldn't help but point out all the other kids who were carrying their bags. "But they just have skates and little pads in them. I've got a lot more than them."

"You can handle it." Bishop tried not to laugh but Bella needed to learn the responsibility that came with playing a sport. As soon as they made it inside and everyone was gearing up, Bella got over the fact that he wouldn't carrying her bag in. She was just as excited as the rest of the kids. Bishop sat in the stands on the outside of the crowd of parents. He got to see her wobble out on to the ice. He couldn't be more proud of her when he watched her start in warm-ups.

The kids were all over the ice during the sharks and minnows game. Bella was fast on her skates despite the pads she was wearing, avoiding being tagged and becoming a shark. Ivy seemed to delight in the fact she was a shark and got to go after other minnows. She was going to make one hell of a defensive player.

"My kid is a literal shark." Barrett groaned as he sat down next to Bishop. His thigh pressed along Bishop's and their ankles bumped together anytime either of them shifted. Barrett dug out a pair of granola bars and offered one to Bishop, which he took gratefully. "She's enjoying chasing the other kids way too much. It's like she knows she can scare the ever-loving daylights out of everyone by growling at them as she barrels down the ice."

"Yeah, I think Ivy might be the one starting a few fights on ice," Bishop admitted.

"Bella will be yelling down the ice encouraging her." Barrett laughed and shook his head. "Why did we agree to put them in hockey?"

"Because we're crazy," Bishop answered. "At least they're getting to start with something fun. I figure they're going to be doing a lot of drills to figure out their skill sets and then Thursday's practice is going to be the one they come home exhausted from."

"Oh, you're going to be one of those hockey dads," Barrett joked.

"No, I'm trying not to. I want her to have fun, but I have a hard time turning off the professional player part of my mind," Bishop admitted sheepishly. "I wanted to get her with a goalie coach, but it's eight and under. I'm not doing that to her. If she asks then that will be completely different, but hockey probably won't be her life like it became mine."

"It's killing you not to be out on the ice coaching her, isn't it?" Barrett grinned.

"No," Bishop lied. "Not at all."

"You have a game Thursday," Barrett pointed out. "Do you need me for Bella duty?"

"If you don't mind?" Bishop grimaced. "I could probably talk Andy's wife into watching her but she might miss practice."

"I can handle it." Barrett shrugged a shoulder. "You've got what, another week or so before your sitter is available?"

"Yes, thank goodness."

"Hey!" Barrett protested. "I think I do a great job watching her."

"You do!" Bishop backtracked. "I just hate feeling like I'm taking advantage of you."

"I'm just messing with you. I know what you mean. I hated having to rely on my mom always watching Ivy when she was a baby and I was getting my life together."

"Exactly." Bishop nodded his head. "I should have everything figured out but shit still happens and you end up in a bind."

One of the other parents glared at him for the use of profanity, but he could only roll his eyes. If they knew the words that would come out of their own mouths during games, they wouldn't give them such a dirty look. Plus, none of the kids could hear him and there weren't any kids hanging around them either.

"What about her Mom?" Barrett asked.

"She's not in the picture." Bishop shrugged a shoulder. "She couldn't handle both a baby and an AHL hockey player. I don't blame her, I was a jerk and thought my job should have come first. It took two months by myself, and sobbing to my best friend Nate and my mom every night to realize how wrong I had been. She sends Bella birthday cards, gifts and the like, but she has her life in New York now. I've got one hundred percent custody of Bella and it works out well for us. I wouldn't ever stop her mom from visiting if she asked, but she never does."

"Ah," Barrett nodded. "Ivy sees her Mom off and on throughout the year. We do holidays and birthdays and everything together, but Ivy stays with me full time. Claire and I were better off friends. One night of experimentation lead to the best thing in my life."

A loud sound of a puck smacking the glass broke their conversation as they both looked up to see who had put that much force behind a pass. Ivy was bright red, her stick on the ice and her gloved hands covering her mouth in surprise. Bishop burst out laughing and clapped Barrett on the shoulder. "I foresee lots of cracked house siding and dents in your car that have to be taken care of in the future."

Barrett buried his face in his hands, his cheeks just as red as Ivy's. "I wasn't expecting that."

"I don't think she was either." Bishop chuckled.

It was fun watching the girls go through the motions. The agility drills had a few of the girls face planting as they attempted to jump and run over the lined up sticks on the ice. Everyone's favorite stations were at the end of practice. The puck control station that ended up with Bella trying to block their shots in goal, shooting against the boards to work on wrist shot technique and the keep away station. While they watched, Bishop tucked the last bit of their conversation away to visit later. He was stuck on the word 'experimentation'. Did that mean what he interpreted it to mean? Could Barrett be gay or bisexual? He might have wanted it to mean that and he was manipulating everything to point in the direction that said Barrett was attracted to men. Barrett could be attracted to him.

He tuned back in to the end of practice huddle where the coaches told the girls they would play ten minute cross-ice game against each other. He felt his stomach drop. He was going to miss it. They hadn't received their game schedule and he hoped that he'd make it to her first game and as many as he could after that. He wanted her to have what he did when he was a kid. His mom or dad in the stands, watching him train. They always knew what to say after a hard loss and when to push him to work harder. Bishop looked over to Barrett not sure how to ask him for more. He didn't need to though. Barrett held his phone up with a kind smile. "Do you want me to FaceTime or record it?"

"Please?" Bishop asked sweetly.

"Like I'd let you miss it."

"Thank you," Bishop breathed out. He wasn't sure what he had done in a past life to deserve Barrett in his life. It only served to add to the attraction Bishop felt towards him.

"I wouldn't want to miss it either. I know you would do the same thing for me if I asked," Barrett said as he stood up to stretch. Even bundled up in a hoodie and a toque on his head Bishop wanted to get his hands on Barrett. They walked side-by-side down to the dressing room. Most of the girls were already out of their pads and back into their regular clothes. Bella was not. She had kicked a skate off out with a huff. "I can't get them off."

Ivy was sitting next to her, her tongue poking out of the corner of her mouth as she tried to help Bella. "Stop moving. I've almost got it. Why did you have to knot it like this?"

"It's how my dad ties his laces," Bella grumbled. "There are too many buckles. Why are there so many?"

Ivy looked up at Bella clearly annoyed by how whiny she had become. "Come on, you can do it. If you can't, I guess that means Adam will get to be starting goalie and then we'll lose every game."

"I won't let us lose," Bella grumbled and took a deep, calming breath as she worked the buckles free. It took her a few minutes but she got it. She looked up and spotted Bishop and Barrett watching them. She frowned, but pulled off the rest of her gear without problem. The pads were frustrating because they were new and the straps hadn't lost that new gear stiffness. The more she practiced putting on her gear, the faster and easier it would be.

" Thanks, Ivy," Bella whispered as they both packed their gear away.

Ivy beamed. "You're welcome. Thursday is going to be awesome."

"I'm going to block all the shots!"

"Not mine!" Ivy shot back.

They walked back to their cars, keeping close to each other and Bishop could get used to that, with the girls scooting along between him and Barrett after hockey practice. Now if he would only get the courage to make it a possibility.

• CHAPTER 13 •

The game had ended and media were still crammed into the locker room, but that didn't stop Bishop from answering the FaceTime call he received from Barrett. He knew the girls were at the end of their practice and he needed to see this. He was out of his skates, but still half way in his gear when he edged off to the back corner.

"Hey. It's loud in here but I can see everything," Bishop said as soon as Barrett said hi and pointed the camera to face the ice. He could hear Barrett's commentary and his loud cheers for Ivy and Bella. It made him excited that Bella had someone there cheering as loudly for her as he would have.

He was watching the girls skating across the ice and Bella stretched out her leg and then reached out to catch the puck in her glove. He jumped with excitement and let out a loud whoop. All the attention of the locker room that had been focused on Morry detailing their win, shot over towards him. His skin flushed and he could hear Barrett laughing in the background.

"What's happening over there?" Preacher questioned.

"Bella's first scrimmage," Bishop admitted. The lights from the cameras blinded him. He doubted the footage would hit television screens but he wanted to share her success. "She's a goalie for her eight and under team. Look."

He turned the phone in order for everyone else to see. The girls were still skating back and forth across the ice trying to get a point. Bella was making it hard for them.

"Is that Ivy?" Tony asked pointing to the blond braid flowing from underneath her helmet. "She wasn't kidding when she said you were her favorite. She plays like you. Vicious."

"Your daughter is a goalie?" One of the reporters asked.

"She sure is." Bishop grinned. "She's definitely been practicing when I wasn't looking."

He turned the phone back facing him and he laughed at one of the girl's cellies after they scored on Bella. There had been a lot of jumping and shaking going on. He loved seeing how excited and happy they had all been. When they got into a game he knew they would be focused and serious, but here in practice they got to have fun.

"I wish I would have recorded Bella warming up. She's been working on her butterfly stretch in her gear.

She ended up slipping on the ice and Ivy tried to help her up. They were a mess."

"Thank you," Bishop rubbed at his eyes. "Tell the girls we scored one for each of them. I've got to go. There are a lot of cameras and you might be famous in the morning. My bad."

The entire locker room burst out laughing as Bishop ended the call and looked up at the sheepishly. "I'm going to get in so much trouble for being on my phone with you guys in here."

"I think you deserve a pass," the reporter commented. "I think any of the guys would have done the same thing. That's got to be exciting to have a daughter interested in hockey."

"It is," Bishop agreed. "If she would have asked to play hopscotch professionally I'd be there too. I just, I'm proud of her."

"You'll have to keep us updated on her team's progress. But let's get back to the work you and Preacher did on the ice during the second period. That was some fantastic work."

It didn't take long for the media to clear out once everyone focused. Bishop rushed through his shower and got in to his suit. They'd have a night at the hotel and then an early morning to make their way home. He was ready to get home and to see Bug.

He was typing out a quick text message to check in with Barrett when Morry sat down next to him on the bus. It wasn't often that the captain graced him with his presence. Immediately Bishop became anxious wondering how much trouble he was going to get into for having his phone out like that.

"You're all over the internet." Morry passed his phone over to let Bishop see what he meant.

Bishop Briggs watching his goalie daughter via FaceTime after the 4-1 victory over the Crusaders.

He watched the video attached with the sound on low. It wasn't anything bad, but there were a lot of women responding how cute it was to see a hockey player excited over youth hockey. He stopped reading after the first comment that made him feel guilty for being a single dad and a professional hockey player at the same time.

"It's not that bad," Bishop pointed out.

"I didn't think so either, but you might get put in the spot light for a while. My wife said, and I quote, 'that was beyond adorable'. You might be fielding personal questions more than hockey questions for a little while. I wasn't sure how that would sit with you," Morry explained.

"It is what it is," Bishop answered with a shrug. "It'll be different, but Tony gets questions about his boys all the time. I can pick his brain about how to navigate it if things get too invasive."

"Good." Morry clapped him on the back. "I did my captainly duty and now I'm going to sit in my spot because it's weird sitting back here by you."

"Oh, thanks. I appreciate it, Cap." Bishop rolled his eyes and focused on his phone to read the text that had come through from Barrett.

"You have to stop looking so good on camera. It's not fair to the rest of us out here."

He sent an eye roll emoji back.

"Seriously. Not fair."

Bishop sent back, *"You can have them all. I'm not interested in any of them."*

His response was fast. *"Then who?"*

Bishop shifted in his seat and looked around the bus to see if anyone was paying attention to what he was doing. Most of the guys were locked on to their phones or listening to music. Trevor had dozed off already. That was ridiculous. He wished he could fall asleep as fast as Trevor could.

"There's this great guy but with my luck, he's unavailable." Bishop typed out and wished he had any idea how to flirt. It seemed like Barrett might be flirting with him.

"You should just ask him. If he says no then he's stupid." Barrett sent back.

"Why?" Bishop asked.

"Stop fishing for compliments. I know you have mirrors in your house asshole."

Bishop burst out laughing at Barrett's response. He glanced over his shoulder to see if he bothered anyone, but everyone was still doing their own thing. He smiled down at his phone and sent back a quick goodnight before hopping off the bus and making his way to his hotel room. He would rather let things linger as they were than to make a mistake and ruining what they had.

• CHAPTER 14 •

Things had changed between Bishop and Barrett. When he picked up Bella he found himself wrapped in a long hug. If he had been more selfish, he would have held on tightly and stayed in Barrett's arms as long as he wanted to. He pulled back, grabbed some of Bella's bags and made his way home. He glanced over his shoulder before closing the front door to see Barrett still standing on his porch watching them.

He didn't want to think about anything other Barrett, but knew that Taryn, the new sitter, would be stopping by to introduce herself to Bella and to get a handle on all the routines and activities they did. He went through the motions with Bella of making sure her gear was stored properly. He talked about how school was going with Bella as he scanned through her folder and graded papers. He signed what he needed to sign and tucked the folder back in her backpack.

Taryn stopped by to meet he and Bella. She was tiny with dark hair and bright blue eyes. She was energetic, creative and had been kind. Both he and Bella liked her. She listened and asked all the right questions. She had been a long term sitter for other professional sports players and she was okay with the hectic schedule. She didn't mind getting the girls to hockey practice if Barrett needed a break from it. He was glad that the team only had one away game before the two upcoming home games. He'd be able to gauge if Bella was comfortable enough to have Taryn sit for her during the longer stretches of time while the team was on the road. If it wasn't a good fit, he needed to find someone to replace her quickly.

Taryn followed them to hockey practice to let her get a hang of getting Bella to practice with enough time to get geared up. She was bundled up in a hoodie, toque and her hands were tucked deep into her pockets.

"I usually walk her to the dressing room and then head over to the stands to watch. Some of the mom's bring books or their iPad with them to read during the practice," Bishop explained. He took his usual seat and noticed that every mom in the rink kept trying to get a good look at Taryn and figure out who she was. Barrett came in and made to sit a few rows up once he spotted Bishop sitting with Taryn. He didn't even bother saying hi, but Bishop stopped him. "Barrett, I wanted you to meet Bella's new sitter. This is Taryn. Taryn, this is Barrett Griffin. He lives next door. His daughter Ivy, the one with the blond braids, is Bella's best friend. He's my, well he's Barrett. I'm trying to show her some of the ropes before leaving in the morning."

"Oh." Barrett stepped down to sit next to Bishop. He offered a smile and his hand to Taryn. "It's good to meet you."

"You too!" Taryn smiled wide. "Mr. Briggs has talked a lot about you and Ivy. I feel like I know more about you two than I do about Bella. I'm sure if I have any questions or need any help, you will be there person to go to."

"Sure, whatever you need." Barrett nodded. "I'm sure he'll give you the same notebook of phone numbers as he gave me."

Taryn laughed. "No doubt. Mr. Pritchard gave me the scoop and told me all about you. I think it's great that even when you're on the road, you make the time to talk to Bella. His wife sent me a text with the footage of you watching her during the scrimmage."

"Well, I'm her dad." Bishop shrugged a shoulder a little embarrassed. "It's what I do."

After that they chatted about the routines and what Bishop's schedule was going to be like the next week. Once the girls were finished Taryn headed home from the rink and Bishop invited Barrett and Ivy over for pizza.

The conversation was subdued between Bishop and Barrett. The girls were chatter boxes as they ate. It made

Bishop feel like he had done something wrong, but he wasn't sure what it could have been. Bishop sent Bella to her room to put away her gear and then she needed a bath. Ivy went with her to help. He gathered up the paper plates and napkins to throw away. He turned and found himself toe to toe with Barrett. "Oh, I'm sorry."

He stood frozen beneath Barrett's gaze. Barrett had bit his lip and looked as if he were about to rethink whatever was on his mind but didn't. He grabbed the plates and napkins from Bishop's hands set it all back on the table, caging Bishop in. He lifted his hand to rest against Bishop's neck. "Tell me if I've been reading this all wrong."

Bishop breathed out a soft, "No."

"Good." Barrett leaned in and pressed his lips against Bishop's. He shifted and set his other hand on Bishop's hip to pull him closer. It was a rush, being this close to another man. To have the heat of Barrett's hands against his skin and the way he parted their lips made his heart pound in his chest. He felt Barrett's chest surge up against his as he pressed to his toes to make up for the height difference. Bishop kept him there, his hands at the small of Barrett's back urging for more that.

The chatter of the girls making their way back towards the kitchen pulled them apart. Bishop was embarrassed to admit that he wanted to reach out to pull Barrett back just to get one last taste. Barrett reached up to fix Bishop's hair. He grabbed the plates and tossed them in the trash and Bishop looked for something to do other than stand in the middle of the kitchen.

"We're going home?" Ivy asked as she grabbed her cup off the table and finished the last dregs of her juice off.

"Yeah, because you stink." Barrett poked Ivy in the side causing her to laugh.

"I do not." Ivy giggled as he found her ticklish spot.

Barrett looked up with a grin, "Have a good night. Sweet dreams, Bella."

"Good night, Mr. Griffin!" Bella yelled over her shoulder as she made her way to the bathroom.

Bishop walked them to the door. Barrett stopped and turned to face him, "Hey, have a safe flight tomorrow. Let me know when you land?"

"Sure." Bishop watched until he got a wave from Barrett as they disappeared inside.

"What are you smiling like that for, Dad?" Bella asked.

"I'm smiling because it's been a good night," Bishop explained as he nudged her towards the bathroom. "Get in the tub and clean up. Ms. Taryn will be here early tomorrow to get you on the bus. I have to leave before you wake up but I'll call as soon as you get out of school."

"How long are you going to be gone?" Bella asked.

"Three days tops. I fly out in the morning, then we have a practice skate that evening and the next day is the game. We're supposed to be flying home right after," Bishop answered.

"Okay." Bella nodded. "You're going to miss my practice."

"I know." Bishop sighed. "But I'll have Barrett record you in goal. That way I won't have to miss anything."

"Good." Bella nodded again. "You'll be at the game?"

"You bet I'll be there." Bishop pressed a kiss to her forehead. He watched as she made her way into the bathroom. He listened as she sang to herself. Tonight had been a good night. He got to see Bella and Ivy practice, they had dinner together and then Barrett. He smiled to himself. If that kiss was a sign of what was to come, he didn't want to wait.

CHAPTER 15

Preacher was barely awake when he sat down next to Bishop on the plane. He reached for Bishop's coffee and finished it off. When Bishop didn't offer any kind of argument for that he raised a brow, "Something is different about you."

"I actually slept last night," Bishop suggested.

"It's still night," Preacher grumbled.

"No," Bishop made a point of checking his watch, "it's six in the morning."

"And you never smile until you put Bella on the bus. It's a rule." Preacher opened his eyes all the way. It took him a few minutes before he grinned. "Something happened with Barrett didn't it?"

Bishop kept his lips pressed together so not to say anything. He knew what Preacher was like. As soon as he got wind of something interesting, he had to tell the entire team. He couldn't keep a secret.

"Oh," Preacher said and every word after that became louder than the one before it . "Did you two do it?"

"Shut the fuck up." Bishop smacked a hand over Preacher's mouth, but the damage was done. Trevor and Tony heard.

"Bishop got some?" Trevor turned around in his seat to look at them. He looked around the cabin of the plane and smacked Morry's shoulder. "Bishop made a move."

Morry blinked the fog of sleep from his eyes and he still didn't comprehend what they were saying. "What?"

"He just kissed me," Bishop hissed out. Two seconds later he regretted saying anything. Preacher had gotten loud as he shoved at Bishops shoulder.

"This is happening." Preacher wiped an imaginary tear from the corner of his eye. "I thought you were going to die a virgin."

"Because Bella was totally an immaculate conception." Bishop rolled his eyes. "You're such a dick. That's why I didn't say anything in the first place."

"Hey." Preacher stood up, "How much do you want to bet that it takes another year for Bishop to hit that?"

"I bet two months," Tony piped up.

"No," Archer disagreed. "It'll be sooner than that. I've seen the way he looks at you. Like a lion about to eat a zebra."

Preacher looked over at Bishop and mouthed, "A zebra?"

"What the fuck?" Bishop twisted in his seat to look at Archer.

"Just saying," Archer shrugged. "I know these things."

Bishop was cut off from saying anything else when they went through the take-off procedures. By the time they were in the air, most of the guys had automatically switched over to their usual flight routines. It wasn't a long flight, a little over four hours to make it to Dallas. Bishop took advantage of the quite flight and napped. He would have enough to think about when they landed. They'd be heading straight to lunch and then to afternoon skate. It would be nonstop when the made it to Texas.

$

He had sent a quick text to Barrett and Taryn letting them know that he had arrived safely in Dallas. He reminded Taryn that tonight was a hockey night and to make sure Bella ate before practice and to have a filling snack before bed. Barrett sent him a text back saying, "Next time stop by before you leave," followed by a winking emoji.

"I wouldn't want to be woken up at four in the morning to say goodbye," Bishop sent back.

"Who said I was going to say goodbye?"

Well, that sent Bishop's mind in a tailspin. Maybe the next trip he would take Barrett up on that. The thought made him pause. Neither of them had really talked about what this meant. It could have just been a moment and that's all the kiss would ever be. But the way Barrett was flirting made Bishop think there was a chance for a relationship. He needed to make a call. They guys were heading into the restaurant for lunch. There would been enough time for him to make a quick call to see what Nate thought about the situation. He scrolled through his contacts and called Nate.

"Hey, man. How are you doing?" Nate asked as he answered the phone.

"I'm good. We made it to Dallas and we're about to head to lunch before skate," Bishop said. "How are you and Roman doing?"

"Good! We're doing really well. It gets difficult every now and then while we're on the ice and someone goes after him but we deal with it as it comes," Nate answered. "What about you? I saw that clip of you watching Bella block a goal. When I showed Roman he told me, 'Okay, now I see what you saw in him'. Don't make me fight you on the ice when we play against each other in a month."

"Like you would be fast enough to land a hit," Bishop chirped.

"Is that a challenge?" Nate teased.

"We'd end up laughing our asses off before either of us managed to throw a punch and you know it." Bishop rolled his eyes.

"What's going on that you decided you needed to call?" Nate asked.

"You know my next door neighbor, Barrett?"

"Oh yeah, I remember him. You won't shut up about how majestic he is. Like a lost fucking unicorn."

"I'm not that bad," Bishop protested.

"Sure, like you didn't write me shitty songs when we dated." Nate chuckled.

"You said you loved those songs!" Bishop pointed out.

"Cause you wrote them. I didn't say they were any good."

"Whatever. See if I try to do anything nice for you ever again." Bishop rolled his eyes.

"Tell me all about Barrett. I've got time," Nate said seriously.

"Well he kissed me and flirts with me and I'm not sure what that all means," Bishop said in a rush.

"Wait, he kissed you and you're actually flirting? Damn, I need to tell Roman about this. Where is he when I need his witty ass?"

"Can you not?" Bishop grumbled.

"Okay, okay. What makes you unsure of what's going on between you two?"

"He kissed me last night and then I had to fly out this morning. We didn't have time to talk about it. Then he text me saying I should have said goodbye this morning, at four in the morning."

"You are just as bad as you were when we were kids. It took you a month before you believed that I was into you. How many times did I kiss you before you got the message?" Nate snorted. "He's into you and he's flirting with you. He made a move and now it's your turn. Don't dance around this like you always do. You like Barrett. Go for it."

"What if by the time I get back in town he realizes it's a mistake?"

"Then you move on and keep doing what you always do," Nate offered. "It's not like it'll be the end of the world."

"But—" Bishop scratched at the back of his neck.

"No buts," Nate interrupted. "I know how you are. Get out of your head and just go with the flow. None of this has to be traditional or perfect. Hell, look at me and Roman. It took us years and now I can't get enough of that jerk. We get mad at each other over stupid shit, but we work through it. If you like him, you'll put the effort into it just like he will."

"I suck at relationships," Bishop groaned.

"You kind of do," Nate laughed. "You should have fun with it. And if it turns out that you're just two dudes buddy fucking, then that's what it is. You never know if you don't go for it."

"I should have just asked Preacher what to do."

"He would have told you man up and go for it. I don't know why you like that dude. He's a dick."

"To anyone who isn't on his team." Bishop laughed.

"You should go for it though," Nate said. "If I wouldn't have tried with Roman I wouldn't be as happy as I am. Go for it. I mean, he put me through some shit that I'll never let him live down, but it's been worth it."

"Fine, but if I fuck things up I'm blaming you." Bishop didn't bother waiting to hear Nate's response. He ended the call and checked his watch. If he didn't get his ass into the restaurant he would be at the mercy of whatever Preacher ordered for him. The last time he got a seafood dish from hell. He wasn't going through that again. He took his seat next to Preacher and shook his head at the drink that was waiting for him.

It was pink with a slice of pineapple on the brim and topped off with an umbrella. Bishop raised a brow, smelled the drink before taking a sip of it to see what they ordered him. He liked the fruity taste of it. They were even kind enough to order it alcohol free.

"Do I want to know what this is called?"

"Nope," Archer answered as the rest of the team laughed around him. He scooted the extra glass of water he had as his elbow over to Bishop. "Who were you talking to? The Bugster is still at school or was she sick?"

"No, she's fine. I was talking to Nate."

"Fuck him," Preacher grumbled. "He's a dick."

Bishop pressed his lips together to stop himself from laughing. He would never understand why they hated each other, but at least they were civil to each other off the ice.

Bishop hated Dallas and the way the fans hissed when they took to the ice. It's bad enough when the Wolves fans howled at the top of their lungs, but nothing compared to that hiss. It made the hair on the back of his neck stand up. It didn't make it any better when they ended up with a power play within the first two minutes of the game. Trevor needed to watch his skates and stop pulling pointless tripping penalties.

It always felt like he took hits harder and was more tempted to throw down his gloves down here. They were cocky and someone needed to knock them down a peg or two. It got rough after the first period of play. The Rattlers were being reckless and if they messed with Archer one more time in goal, there was no letting that go. The first time could be passed off as an honest mistake. Bishop wasn't going to let another mistake go. He didn't care if Jannik Müller was a giant on ice. He'd go for it.

Bishop knew he was going to drop gloves when Müller skated by him with a toothy grin. "Can't protect your goalie, can't score a point. What good are you Briggs?"

He shoulder checked Bishop hard and pushed off after the puck. As he and Preacher skated towards the other end of the ice they shared a look. Preacher gave him a subtle nod, as if to say he had Bishop's back. He wasn't going to go after Müller behind the net. He'd wait until they go to the face-off circle. It was worth the wait. Müller crashed into Archer and the Referees were shoving and pushing players away from each other. The puck was declared dead and they set up at the dot. Bishop shook his hands out and as soon as the puck drop he threw his gloves and stick to the ice to go after Müller. He slammed a fist just under the visor of Müller's helmet. He grabbed the ugly burnt red jersey and dragged Müller down to the ice. He felt white hot pain at the bridge of his nose but that only served to make him angrier. He got on top of Müller and shoved his face into the ice. "You either cut that shit out, stay away from the fucking goal or we go another fucking round."

Müller laughed as he squirmed underneath Bishop. "You're out of this game, you know that right?"

Bishop growled when he was tugged off of Müller. There was a vague sense of satisfaction seeing Müller dazed as he wobbled and skated towards the benches. Bishop watched as he made his way down the tunnel to get checked over. He wiped at the bridge of his nose and grabbed his helmet as he headed towards the benches. He knew he was out for the rest of the game but he knew the Rattlers would stay away from Archer. Mission accomplished.

Bishop got fist bumps from the guys on the edge of the bench and a few from fans leaning over the stand barriers. The adrenaline coursing through his veins kept him from feeling any pain. He was surprised when medical came in with a stitch kit. Three stitches across the slope of his nose and onto his cheek. He kept quiet as medical cleared him and managed to shower before the rest of the guys got in from the end of the game. He grinned as they made their way into the locker room. A fight and a win. That makes for one hell of a night. The only thing that would have made it better was if this was a home game and he was going home to Barrett.

• CHAPTER 16 •

It was just after ten when Bishop made it home. He set his clothes to wash and made his rounds around the house. He made sure Bella had been keeping up with her chores and didn't throw her gear on the floor in her closet. She had her own system going with storing her gear. They'd end up having to keep things in the garage before long. Being a sweaty mess on ice led to gear that reeked. Taryn left him a note on the counter to keep him updated on Bella. It was a relief seeing that Bella had a nanny who made sure she kept up with her school work and practice. Taryn would be back for the practice and the next home games, unless he needed her before that.

He showered off the stale air of the airplane and changed into a pair of sweats and a worn out tee-shirt. He was planning on a nap and doing nothing until Bella got home. His face had bruised just under his eye and the stitches looked disgusting but it wasn't too bad. He needed to figure out how to tell Bella fighting wasn't okay, even though he fully supported and participated in fighting on the ice. He didn't think he'd have to find a way to explain to Bella that fighting wasn't the answer without sounding hypocritical.

Three quick raps on the door halted any thought of what he needed to talk to Bella about. His heart started to race. There was only one person who could be at his door at eleven in the morning. He almost wished he put on regular clothes rather than planning to lounge around in his sweats. Barrett was leaned back against the porch railing when Bishop opened the door. His long lean legs were crossed in front of him and his arms crossed over his chest. Bishop let his eyes linger on the bulge of muscle and he traced down to the sliver of skin exposed at his hip. He wanted to cross the steps separating them to see if Barrett tasted as good as he looked.

Bishop's voice was rough when he finally spoke, "Hey."

"Aren't you going to invite me in?" Barrett raised a brow.

"Yeah, sure. Come in." Bishop took a step back and Barrett brushed against his chest as he stepped inside. He barely got the door shut before Barrett had pressed him against the wall. His lips parted around a gasp. Barrett leaned in and brushed the tip of his nose against the uninjured side of Bishop's nose and stole a quick kiss. Bishop tilted his head and chased after Barrett's lips. The short, teasing touch wasn't nearly enough. Bishop watched as Barrett licked his lips. Bishop scrubbed a hand up the back of his neck and through his hair. Well, that was one way to say hello.

"Hi." Barrett smiled up at him. "It's good to see you."

"Yeah." Bishop returned the smile, albeit a little more sheepish than Barrett. "You want something to eat? I had just started thinking about food when you knocked on the door."

"Sure." Barrett followed Bishop into the kitchen. He sat at the bar and watched Bishop dig in the cabinets and the fridge as he searched for something to make. They sat quietly and settled on cooking chicken and pasta. It was quick, easy and wouldn't require him to pay too much attention to it.

"How's the nose?" Barrett asked.

"It looks much worse than it is. Müller was itching for a fight and he got it after he messed with Archer one too many times. I couldn't let him get away with it. Otherwise everyone would think they could step in Archer's net. I can't let that happen." Bishop explained.

"When do the stitches come out?"

"Five more days," Bishop answered.

"I might need you to talk to Ivy." Barrett smirked. "She says if anyone messes with Bella she's going to do just what you did."

Bishop's face dropped, "She didn't."

"She even asked if I could put her in karate too. That way she could fight just as good as Mr. Briggs did." Barrett was laughing as he said it.

"I'm sorry." Bishop hid his face in his hands for a moment. "If she does get in a fight, you know Bella will be right there beside her. Goalie or not, she'll jump into the scrum if Ivy's there."

"Those girls wouldn't know what to without each other."

"If I ever get traded it'll break Ivy's heart."

"I wouldn't be too fond of that happening either," Barrett admitted softly.

"So, this," Bishop gestured between himself and Barrett, "it's more than neighbors. Right?"

"I don't know how many neighbors you go around kissing but I only do that when I'm interested in a person. Interested in having a relationship with them."

Bishop busied himself with dishing up their lunch. He carried the dishes over to the breakfast table and gestured for Barrett to take a seat. He handed over the plate before sitting down on the opposite of him. He took a few bites trying to get his thoughts together. "So this isn't just a sex thing?"

Barrett choked and pounded his chest. "No, definitely not."

"I was just checking." Bishop laughed. "Some guys would rather not bother with a relationship. I'm not one of them, but it's better to ask in the beginning then to get things confused."

"So," Barrett drawled out. "Do you want to go on a date with me?"

Bishop grinned. "You should know that I don't put out on the first date."

"Damn." Barrett breathed out a disappointed sigh. "All my plans are ruined. And I was going to put out all the stops. I guess now we'll just hit up the Waffle House and hope for the best."

"I'll only go to Waffle House if you liquor me up first. That's a steadfast rule. Waffle House is for drunken shenanigans."

"Drunken shenanigans," Barrett repeated and shook his head fondly.

"Yes, drunken shenanigans." Bishop repeated as he stood up to put his plate in the sink. He turned back to see that Barrett had spun around in his seat and his eyes were firmly locked on Bishop's ass. Now that he could say with certainty that he and Barrett were going to be more than neighbors, he didn't hesitate to lean down to have the kiss that Barrett had denied him earlier at the door.

He reached down just as Barrett tilted his head back in anticipation of the kiss. His lips were warm and already parted. Bishop licked into Barrett's mouth. He wanted Barrett to stand up to have a better angle. He wasn't able to move as he wanted. The decision was taken out of his hands when he felt Barrett's hands wrap around the back of his thighs and pull him forward. Bishop let Barrett guide him onto Barrett's lap. The position made him want to roll his hips down against Barrett's, he wanted to get his hands one every inch of skin that he could. He let out a groan when Barrett nipped at his lip, his teeth tugging just hard enough to send a jolt of heat racing down his spine.

He tore his lips from Barrett's trying to catch his breath, but Barrett didn't stop. His mouth trailed down Bishop's jaw, stopping just at the base of his throat. He focused on the hollow of his throat. Bishop tapped Barrett on the shoulder, "Hey, stop."

Barrett pressed a kiss to the underside of Bishop's jaw. "What's wrong?"

"Nothing," Bishop answered too quickly.

Barrett took a breath and leaned against the back of the chair looked up at Bishop. "Again, what's wrong?"

"Nothing is wrong," Bishop admitted and he averted his eyes. "I just, I want to go on a date before jumping into bed. If that's what you end up wanting too."

"You have to know I want you in every possible way I can have you." Barrett blew out a breath and tapped Bishop's thigh, "Up."

"I'm sorry. Can we just rewind and pretend the last two minutes didn't happen?" Bishop asked as he stood up.

"Nope, now you have to take me on the greatest date ever." Barrett grinned. "Like, take me to the fancy Waffle House kind of great."

Bishop burst out laughing. It was telling that he knew exactly which one Bishop was talking about. "You mean the one by the church?"

"That's the one." Barrett nodded.

"I don't think we're going to be getting drunk together any time soon but if it happens, we're going to the fancy Waffle House. I'll call Preacher to drive us." Bishop leaned down to press a chaste kiss to Barrett's lips. "Thank you."

"I was getting a little carried away and I have a deadline to meet this evening and I've got five pages left to finish." Barrett admitted. "I just missed you."

Bishop wrapped his arms around Barrett and held him tight. He pressed a kiss to Barrett's cheek before stepping back. "How are you so perfect? Don't answer that, let the mystery stand."

Barrett chuckled before stealing one last, quick kiss and started towards the door. "I'm not perfect. I'll see you later. I'm sure Ivy will try and sneak over after her homework."

"I'll feed her and send her back."

"Bye." Barrett shook his head fondly. Bishop watched as he bounced down the porch steps and turned around with a bright smile. "I'll see you at practice tonight?"

$

Bishop didn't wait long to call Taryn. Despite the fact he felt like it was asking too much of her to sit with both Bell and Ivy while he went out on a date with Barrett. He felt guilty for asking her to give up her evening when he should be spending his time with Bella. Later in the season there wouldn't be as many opportunities and if they made it into the playoffs, then it would be even more hectic for awhile. He didn't want to miss the opportunity to spend time with Barrett just the two of them, but he also didn't want to miss out on anything with Bella.

It was something he had a hard time reconciling within himself. It must have been across his face when

Taryn answered his call. "Hey, Mr. Briggs. Is there a change in the schedule?"

"Oh, there's no change in the schedule. I'm still home and in town." Bishop pressed his lips together in thought. "I need to ask a favor of you."

"Okay, I'm all ears. What do you need?"

"Do you mind taking Bella and Ivy one night that I'm in town? You'll get your usual pay plus some."

"I don't mind. You and Mr. Griffin need a night away from the girls?" Taryn asked.

"Um," Bishop scratched at the back of his neck. "It's more like I want to take him on a date."

"Oh!" Taryn sounded like she had been taken by complete surprise. "I didn't know you two were together."

"Kind of," Bishop answered. "It's new and we haven't actually gone out on a real date. I was hoping that before I left for the next couple of games we could have an evening to ourselves. It would only be a few hours."

"I don't mind at all. Ivy's sweet," Taryn commented. She hummed beneath her breath as if she were thinking over her words and trying to decide what and how she wanted to say it.

"What is it?" Bishop asked.

"Can I ask you a few questions? If you don't want to answer them tell me so and I'll leave you be. I'll keep it all between us, like I promised when I signed the NDA and work agreement."

"Okay, go for it." Bishop made his way to the kitchen table and took a seat. He picked at a sticker Bella had stuck to the table when he wasn't looking.

"You're gay?" Taryn questioned.

"Bisexual," Bishop corrected her. "Is that a problem for you?"

"No, no, of course not," Taryn rushed out. "I just, I thought I would have known."

"I haven't dated much since having Bella. It's a lot of work and then I have my actual work. It barely leaves any time for dating," Bishop admitted. "I haven't been interested in anyone, not like now."

"So who knows?" Taryn asked.

Bishop laughed. "I reckon most everyone knows. I don't hide it all that well. My family, team and friends. They all know. I don't think I would be willing to hide it either. It's kind of like one of the best kept secrets in the league, knowing who is gay and who isn't. There are guys who will use it against you when you're out on the ice, but most of the younger guys don't care. There are a few bad apples and old players who will make a big deal of it, but it's easy to pick them out."

"Well, you don't have anything to worry from me," Taryn promised. "I think love is a beautiful thing and it's amazing when you find it."

"Exactly." Bishop nodded.

"So what night did you need me?" Taryn asked.

"I was thinking Wednesday night? If you didn't have plans. If you do, I can do another day. I don't even know if he wants to go. I haven't actually asked him." Bishop felt his cheeks flush with embarrassment. He was working off the assumption that Barrett wasn't busy with his work and was okay with going on a date.

"Where are you thinking about going?"

"I wanted to try that new steak house downtown, but then it's got a very intimate feeling. Then I thought The Pit, but it's so open and a lot of people there will recognize me and someone is bound to interrupt us." Bishop let out a frustrated sigh.

"How about this," Taryn offered. "You go get take-out or cook something nice for him at his house while I watch the girls here."

"I don't want him to think I don't want to be seen out in public with him and I kind of want to take him out."

"I think you're worrying way too much. Maybe go to the Brew House in Towne Center. I think that would be perfect for you two. No major sports game going on to fill it to the brim and it's a Wednesday night. It'll be great," Taryn explained.

"Why are you so awesome?" Bishop asked. It was nice being able to talk this through and to figure everything out with someone who wasn't going to make fun of him the whole time like Preacher or Nate would do.

Taryn laughed, "I don't think I'm awesome, but thank you. You're going to have to let me know if Wednesday works for him or if you'll need me another day."

"If you're ever interested in anyone on the team or the ice crew, you let me know. I'll set you up in a heart-beat. You are an angel." Bishop stood up.

Taryn laughed, "Okay. Well on that note, I'm going to go. I've got some errands to run. You let me know about that date."

"I will," Bishop said as he hung up. He dropped his head to the table with a relieved sigh. He had a babysitter figured out and now he had to see if Wednesday evening would work for Barrett. He padded back into the living room to see Bella watching television and halfway working on her homework. "If you don't get your homework done, there's no hockey practice for you."

Bella looked up at him with wide eyes and a protest on her tongue. Bishop cut her off before she could get started. "You know the rules, school and then sports."

"Fine," Bella grumbled. "I'm almost done anyway."

He watched as Bella turned the television off in order to focus on her work. He glanced out the window towards Barrett's house. He'd have a chance tonight to talk to him without the girls getting in the way. It wasn't ideal but he figured asking him at the rink was as good of a time as any.

$

Bishop had gotten used to Bella running off as soon as they got into the rink for the locker room. She always had to be one of the first on the ice and with all her gear she had to put on, she didn't waste any time. He made the trek to the stands with his hands tucked in his pockets and looking for Barrett. He must not have arrived yet so he scoped out the perfect seats that sat at an angle so they could see up and down the ice without much in the way.

A to-go cup of coffee hovered in front of Bishop's face before he realized that Barrett had made it in. He took the coffee with a smile. "Thanks."

"How was your day?" Barrett asked as he pressed closer to Bishop on the bench.

"Good." Bishop nodded. "Practice was hell. My legs are still screaming from the work we put in today. What about you?"

Barrett flexed his hand out. Bishop hadn't noticed it earlier, but Barrett's fingers were covered in faded ink. He even had some on his forearms. He must have put in a lot of time to leave that kind of evidence behind. "I managed to get a lot of inking done today. I made a bit of a mess out of myself."

Bishop smiled at him, "Whatever it takes."

"You ready for your next game?" Barrett asked.

"Yeah," He nodded. "The next couple of games are in town. It'll be nice to be able to stick around and catch Bella's first game before having to head off to travel for a while."

"Anything planned for while you're hear or are you just going to do the usual stuff you always do?"

"I have training between the games but I was actually wanting to talk to you about possibly doing something Wednesday night. Just me and you. Taryn said she'd be happy to watch Ivy while she watches Bella."

Barrett smiled, "Are you asking me on a date?"

Bishop tapped his fingers on his knees, "Maybe."

"No kids? Just you and me?"

"Yes," Bishop confirmed.

"What are we going to do on this date?" Barrett asked. "Please tell me it's the fancy Waffle House."

"If you give me an answer I'll tell you what we're going to do on our date," Bishop teased.

"Wednesday?"

"Or whenever you're free."

"You know even if I wasn't free on Wednesday I'd work around it so I could go on a date with you, right?" Barrett bumped his shoulder against Bishop's. "I would. Where are we going to go?"

"I was thinking dinner at the Brew House?" Bishop threw out the suggestion and hoped that it would be a good choice. After Taryn had suggested it, he saw the appeal of it. It wouldn't be filled with people and it wasn't too intimate. It was the perfect medium.

"That sounds good to me," Barrett answered.

"Good." Bishop tucked his hands into the pockets of his sweater. He wanted to wrap an arm around Barrett's shoulders, but knew this wasn't the time or place. The thwack of a hockey puck hitting the glass served as a reminder of where they were. His attention shifted from Barrett and out onto the ice to see Bella practicing her stretches with her goalie partner and coach. Ivy was flying up and down the ice with her blond braid flowing out from beneath her helmet.

He caught Barrett watching him off and on through-out the practice. He was sure Barrett caught him doing the same thing but he couldn't stop himself. He didn't want to stop himself. Now that he was welcome to look his fill he couldn't seem to stop himself.

$

The clothes hanging in his closet were judging him. Bishop couldn't figure out what he should wear and the clothes hanging in the closet were judging him for his lack of decision making skills. He hadn't been on a date since Bella was born. He had hookups here and there but it was never anything he was serious about. It was never anyone he wanted to impress and keep around that would cause his nerves to get this out of control. He was glad that Taryn had already collected the girls for their own dinner and movie night. Otherwise his nerves would have been a million times worse.

He finally decided on casual. They were friends be-fore they got to this point. He wanted to put in the effort, but not look ridiculous. He grabbed his black jeans and a button up shirt that he rolled the sleeves up to his elbows. It would work. He decided against shav-ing for tonight. There was something about the way Barrett's eyes lingered along his jaw this morning at the bus stop with the girls that may have been the deciding factor in his decision. He checked his watch and knew he needed to grab his keys, walk across the yard and pick Barrett up.

He knocked on the door and rocked back and forth on his feet as he waited for Barrett to answer. When he did, Bishop wanted to skip the date all together. Barrett's hair was styled and his eyes were bright behind his glasses. His shirt stretched across his chest and shoulders showing off the muscle he had. It was more than his lose tee-shirts led Bishop to believe.

"You ready to go?" Barrett smiled softly up at Bishop.

"Yeah. Are you good with me driving?" Bishop asked.

"Sure." Bishop grabbed his keys to lock the door. They walked side-by-side to Bishop's truck and they were quick as he navigated his way on to the highway. Bishop couldn't handle the quiet much longer. "How's your work going?"

"Oh it's been going well. There have been a couple of rewrites so I've had to adjust and redraw, but I think it's only going to make the entire storyline better."

"Am I ever going to get to know anything about the storyline or am I going to have to keep coming up with my own ideas?" Bishop asked.

"You're going to kill me."

"No, I'm not," Bishop insisted.

"It's based on a prep school, which I had no idea those existed until I started Googling them, and the journey of a newer hockey team finding themselves and making it to a larger play off stage."

"So why would I kill you?"

"It's an entirely different league," Barrett stated. "A different skill level and I feel like I may have used you just a little bit."

Bishop laughed, "You didn't use me."

"I still feel like I may have because the experience is different. I've fixed the whole, 'they're all dumb jocks who hate people who don't feast on protein shakes' vibe I had going on."

He pressed his lips together to stop himself from laughing at Barrett. "You know that I went to one of those prep schools, right? It is an intense experience. Some people get to board at the school while others have to stay with people they've never met."

"What was it like for you?"

"I loved it. I made a lot of friends and learned who I was without being afraid of people judging me. All they cared about up there was how I played hockey. You come to depend on your friends while you're there. If you're sick and your parents aren't answering their phone to help you figure out what medicine to take, your best friend will find out for you. Anyway, they use the same moves we do. We've just perfected and crafted them to our current positions on the ice better. Most of the kids who go to those schools, end up in one of the big leagues around the globe. I've seen a lot of guys go to the Kontinental Hockey League or to the Swedish Hockey League if they don't find a team here."

Barrett nodded, "I'm learning there is a lot more to hockey than what you see on the surface."

"Enough about me and enough about hockey." Bishop chuckled. "Tell me more about your work. I know you started out with illustrating children's books. What made you jump into graphic novels?"

"I got the opportunity to work with someone on a story line, instead of only drawing for something that had already been written. I've always wanted to be able to get more involved in the creative process. Being able to work hand in hand with someone on a project, it's what I've always wanted to do," Barrett answered. "I get to travel and meet so many different people. Not everyone gets opportunities like that. If I would have done anything else career wise, I don't think I would have been as happy as I am."

"Exactly!" Bishop said excitedly. "That's how I feel about it."

"Tell me about your family?" Barrett asked.

He lost track of time as they drifted further into conversation with Barrett. He didn't have a problem talking about his parents or his brother. He kept in touch with each other regularly and they'd be coming up after Christmas to visit and see Bella. Barrett's family was the opposite. He didn't have the unwavering support like Bishop had. Anytime he spoke with his parents, they'd ask about how his work was going and if he found a job. Bishop could see the hurt in Barrett's eyes and he wanted to do whatever he could to fix that. All he could offer at the moment was to reach out and tangle their fingers together on the table top. When they lapsed into silence, it was comfortable and neither felt a rush to fill it. They were content with quietly watching each other.

Conversation blended into soft tones over a shared desert. Bishop knew that with Barrett, things were different. He wanted to spend as much time as he could with him. It didn't matter if it was two in the morning, if Barrett or Ivy needed him; he knew that he would be there.

Sitting in the driveway, the engine ticking as it cooled, Bishop wanted to ask Barrett inside. He didn't want the evening to end. He looked across the truck to see Barrett toying with his seatbelt, like he was feeling the exact way he was. Excited and unsure all at the same time. It was a rush for Bishop to lean across the center console and reach for Barrett. His fingers slid from the side of his neck around to the soft curls at the nape of his neck. Barrett's eyes fluttered shut. A soft sigh slipped from his lips. Bishop brushed his lips against Barrett's. Once, twice, three times until he didn't want stop himself from lingering.

He could feel Barrett smiling against his lips. The gesture was enough to make him laugh. God, he hadn't felt this light in a long time. It was the perfect was to end the night. They were quiet entering the house and as Barrett managed to wake Ivy up long enough to get her out the door and shuffling across the night damp grass. Bishop waited in the doorway until Barrett had his door unlocked and stepped inside. Barrett waved and mouthed goodnight before heading in.

Curled up against his pillows, Bishop didn't think he would be able to find someone who made him feel the way Barrett managed to after spending a few hours together.

CHAPTER 17

Bishop couldn't get enough of Barrett's kisses. It had become his favorite way to start the morning off. They would get the girls on the bus and then they'd walk over to either of their houses and they would end up wrapped around each other on the couch or find a reason to delay leaving at the front door.

"You're going to be late," Barrett said against Bishop's lips as he leaned back against the couch. Bishop had tried to leave for the rink a few minutes ago, but he got distracted in the front hallway and then they ended up back on the couch. He was cradled between Barrett's thighs and he basked in the attention he was getting.

He didn't care if he ended up being late. Not with the way Barrett rocked into him as he licked into his mouth. Being late would be worth it. One hundred percent. God, there were too many clothes in the way and not enough skin. He let out a breathless moan when Barrett dug his fingers into the flesh of his ass. It was like he couldn't fit enough of it in his palms and he needed to find the perfect hold.

Bishop was close to giving in and skipping skate but he knew what hell that would bring. He pulled away from Barrett's lips and got to his feet. When Barrett made to follow him, Bishop shoved him back down to the couch. "No. I'm already going to get stuck doing bag-skates and puking my guts out because I was late. Don't make it worse."

"Then go." Barrett rolled his eyes. He let his hand rest just above the button of his jeans and fuck, Bishop wanted to stay to see what he had planned. He watched as Barrett's fingers slipped past his waistband and disappeared into his jeans. Instead of facing the pure torture of being late for practice, he stood up, adjusted himself and darted out the door to his truck without bothering to say anything else. If he sped then he might squeak by without being officially late.

He stumbled into the locker room and rushed through getting changed. He could feel the way Morry was watching and waiting for him. Instead of saying anything he laced up and hit the ice right as the rest of the team was starting warm-up stretches.

Preacher raised a brow before saying, "Someone looks like they were having a good time before they decided to join the rest of the team this morning."

"Oh fuck you," Bishop scoffed. "I remember a few times you were much later, showed up still drunk and could barely skate. You don't get to give me any shit."

Preached smiled as he remembered the times Bishop was talking about. "Yeah, it was so worth the shit Morry put me through though."

"Don't let him hear that." Bishop shoved at Preacher's skate blade with his stick, causing him to tip over on the ice.

"You're lucky you're never fucking late. If I would have pulled that shit I'd be skating to my death while everyone else did stretches," Preacher grumbled as he righted himself. "So you and Barrett are going strong?"

"Yeah." Bishop nodded. "It's been good."

"Have you told the girls yet? That you're more than neighborly?" Preacher asked.

Bishop tilted his head back and looked up at the rink lights, "Uh, I'm not sure how or when we're going to approach that."

"Well I think it's something you should put some time into," Preacher pointed out.

"I know. They'll end up walking in on something or wonder why we're spending so much time together." Bishop nodded. "We already get looks from the moms at practice because we only sit by each other or one of us will bring the girls when the other has something they need to do."

"I'm surprised you haven't gotten a shit ton of questions during media," Preacher pointed out.

"Don't get any ideas. If I have to start fielding questions after practice I'll know who pointed the cameras in my direction," Bishop said over his shoulder and effectively cutting off the conversation. He didn't want to know what punishment Morry had up his sleeve if he thought Bishop was slacking.

$

Bishop was exhausted after practice. Morry did think he had been slacking and needed to be reminded that he needed to be on time and not to push it like he did today. He definitely didn't want to have anything to do with the plethora of cameras and reporters he knew were waiting for them. All Bishop wanted was to go home and to take a nap until Bella go home from school.

That was not his luck.

"Bishop, we've got a few questions for you."

He looked over his shoulder and wanted to groan. Seriously? He hadn't even gotten out of his shoulder pads. He sat down and tugged the practice sweater off and started taking his pads off. He wiped his face and focused on the reporter in front of him. "Okay, whenever you're ready."

"What can you do defensively to ensure a win against Boston?"

"We have to get a fast start, put up the first point and keep that momentum. It's going to come down to smart play. Boston is a physical team that likes to push others to pull penalties. We can't afford to play into their hands like that."

There were a few more questions that pertained to playing defensively and keeping their gloves on and avoiding being a man down on the ice. Then the tone shifted and it wasn't about professional hockey, it was about Bella's hockey.

"Your daughter is going to be playing her first game soon. Are you going to get to be there and see it?"

Bishop chuckled, "If everything goes according to plan I'll be there. I might be a little late, but I'm going to be there."

"How is the team handling having her on the team, knowing that you're her dad?"

"They don't make a big deal of it. They know I'm there and who I play for. I think most of the parents are more worried about the havoc Bella and her friend Ivy will cause when Bella isn't in the net." Bishop scratched at the stubble on his chin with a wry grin.

"Has she gotten any extra coaching? I know a lot of families who do that for their kids."

"She's not even seven yet." Bishop wanted to roll his eyes. "She's still learning everything. If she keeps up with it and asks for extra coaching, I'll consider it. But right now she just needs to have fun, focus on school and making friends."

The reporter moved to ask more questions but Bishop cut him off, "I'd love to keep talking about Bella and hockey, but I've got a tight schedule this afternoon."

"Right, well good luck against Boston. We know that you and Preacher will take care of any issues out on the ice."

"For sure." Bishop nodded and waited a few minutes for the media to clear out until he started getting out of the rest of his gear.

"You handled that well," Andy said as he sat down on the bench next to him.

"Is it bad that I don't want them asking about her?" Bishop asked. "There are times I just want to tell everyone in the world about the stuff she's accomplished and other times I want them to butt out."

Andy clapped him on the shoulder, "I completely understand that. The world gets to see different parts of her life but the important stuff? That's only for family."

Bishop nodded, that was exactly what he needed to hear. He wasn't sure how Andy knew he needed that reassurance, but he was glad for it.

• CHAPTER 18 •

Bishop had to rush from the airport but he made it to Bella's first game on time. He wished he would have grabbed his jacket out of the truck, but didn't bother turning back to get it. He wanted to be sure Bella knew he was there. He went straight to the glass and searched her out. He spotted her stretching as Ivy skated in a circle around her talking a mile a minute. He maneuvered his way over so he could knock on the glass to get their attention. Ivy looked up with a huge smile before she got Bella to look over her shoulder. She scrambled up and tugged her helmet off.

"You're here!"

"Of course I'm here!" Bishop grinned. "You two are going to kill it!"

Ivy turned to look in the stands and pointed out where Barrett was. Bishop sent them a thumbs up before heading over to Barrett. He slid into the seat. "I thought I was going to miss it."

Barrett locked their ankles together and smiled, "You're here and that's what matters. How's the hip?"

Bishop didn't want to think about how bruised his hip was. As soon as he did the ache registered in his mind. Despite all the gear he was wearing, the fall he took was bad enough that the medical staff told him he was going to be a scratch for the next week. It was only two games he'd be missing, but it was two games he should be on the ice.

"I'm going to miss the next couple of games," Bishop admitted with a whisper. "Were they nervous?"

"I think Bella was a bit more nervous than Ivy." Barrett said. "She got really quiet on the ride over, but they did a handshake that seemed to brighten things up a bit."

"It's a goalie thing. That intense silence before a game. Archer does the same thing. He sinks into goalie mode," Bishop pointed out. "I didn't think I'd be dealing with that super focus with Bella so soon."

Barrett tensed up when the girls got off the ice and squeezed in together to listen to their coach. It was almost game time. Bella and Ivy were in the starting line-up. It made Bishop proud to see the girls in there with boys who already had a year under their belt. They practiced some aspect of what they had learned with the team at home. They were always challenging and helping each other. He swore Bella was practicing her spelling words in time with her stretches last week.

Barrett's knee was jiggling up and down with nerves as the players skated out for the starting face-off. Bishop set his hand on Barrett's knee to help calm him down. "She's going to do great."

"And if she doesn't, it's not the end of the world," Bishop offered as his eyes tracked the progress the girls were making on the ice. "Remember, it's eight and under. They're supposed to have fun. Right now they're still learning everything."

Barrett laughed. "I thought I would have to be the one reassuring you that winning wasn't everything the entire game."

"Oh! Did you see that pass?" Bishop smacked Barrett on the thigh. It was a beauty of a pass that Ivy made. It gave the team a chance for a goal, but the boy's shot went wide and they were off racing down the ice towards Bella.

Bishop could feel his heart racing as he tracked the puck and glanced down at Bella. She was low, her glove ready and he could only imagine how intense she looked. She managed to get her blocker in position and blocked the goal. He did everything he could not to jump up out of his seat. He gave a yell and clapped with the rest of the parents.

"Oh, you're going to be hell later in the season." Barrett shook his head, laughing softly at Bishop.

"No, I won't," Bishop grumbled. "Some of these moms are going to turn into monsters. You don't have anything to worry about with me."

Bishop smiled down at one of the moms who over heard him and glared at him. She'd be the one who'd try to jump through the glass screaming at the refs. Mid-glare it seemed like she realized who she glared at. Her cheeks flushed and as soon as there was a break in play, she scooted further down the bench.

Barrett did his best to muffle a laugh, "No, you're going to get us in so much trouble. I stand by that."

"Watch the game. Your daughter is about to take that kid out."

"What?" Barrett's head whipped up and he searched the ice for Ivy. She was skating after the puck, by herself. Barrett shoved Bishop, "You're a dick."

Bishop laughed and started to focus one hundred percent on the game playing out in front of them. Bella was doing really well. All that extra work she had put into her stretches, her and Ivy shooting pucks at her after they worked on their spelling words and reading. It was paying off for both of them. It took a little bit of time before either team managed to put up a point, but when they did, the team went wild. Bishop and Barrett were on their feet cheering.

It broke his heart a little to see how upset Bella got from allowing a point, but he was proud of her at the same time. She shook it off, patted the goal posts and refocused. Ivy stuck to her assigned player to cover. Their team managed to secure their first win of the season. Everyone in the stands was on their feet as the team dog-piled on the ice in celebration.

Bishop grabbed Bella's bag to carry with pride. She smiled up at him, "That was awesome!"

"It was!" Bishop nodded. "You were great. Ivy did a great job as well. You played a smart defense."

"Thank you." Ivy smiled up at him. "Does this mean we get to go have pizza?"

Barrett looked over to Bishop asking him without words if this was okay. Bishop shrugged a shoulder, "I can pick some up on the way home."

"Yes!" Bella and Ivy high-fived each other.

"Okay, in the car." Barrett ushered them to his car. He looked up to Bishop, "I've got both of their seats in my car. We can head to my place and you can get the pizza? That way we don't have to go through the trouble of moving them around in the parking lot."

"Sounds like a plan to me." Bishop said as he split up from them and made his way to his truck. He called the order in so he wouldn't have to wait when he picked it up. The selfish part of himself wanted to spend time with just himself and Barrett for a few hours. Instead he had to sit through a hockey game, then a pizza dinner and getting the girls ready for bed before he'd have a few minutes alone with Barrett.

He had barely knocked on the door with the toe of his shoe when the door was opened and Barrett was grabbing the box of pizza out of his hands to set it on the table in the hallway. He tugged Bishop inside by the lapels of his jacket and backed him against the door as he closed it.

Barrett brushed his nose against Bishop's. His lips were parted and his breath was hot against Bishop's lips. Their lips weren't touching, not yet. He had a way of putting the rest of the world on hold and allowed Bishop to focus entirely on the moment happening between the two of them. Everything slowed down and that was when Barrett brushed their lips together. Bishop would never be able to get enough of how plush Barrett's lips were against his.

Cool mint burst across his tongue and it made Bishop smile. The thought that he may have had a mint on the drive home just for this stolen moment between the two of them, it made him itch for more than this. His slid his hands along the small of Barrett's back before moving lower. Barrett's breathing broke and he let Bishops hands urge him closer. Their hips were flush and the slight bit of friction they were managing wasn't going to be enough. It was never enough for Bishop. As his worked his fingers beneath Barrett's sweater and under his shirt, the warmth of his skin made against the pads of his fingertips combined with open mouthed kisses along his jaw made him weak.

"You," Barrett started then stopped. "You just played a hell of a series, got hurt in the process and then you come home to cheer on the girls in this suit. It's not fair that I don't get to take you out of it."

Bishop threw his head back, knocking hard against the door, "You can't say shit like that when we have to face our kids for dinner."

"I'll say it whenever I feel like it," Barrett whispered. He took a step back and Bishop forced himself to look away. If he didn't, he wasn't ever going to make it through the foyer. He kept his head down until he could hear Barrett's soft steps heading towards the living room. He ran his hands through his hair and took a couple of deep breaths before grabbing the pizza and following after him. It was going to be hard going home tonight. The space between their houses felt infinite and he didn't want to make that walk.

They only had a few days before Bishop got cleared for game play and was flying back out for a back to back against DC. They'd be in DC first and then back to play at home. He was missing one of Bella's games. While she'd be in the goal fighting for a win, he was starting his night with warm-ups.

As he made his first round he slowed and cut in front of the net after making sure he wasn't in danger of taking a puck to the head and ran a bare hand along the top of the goal. Archer raised a questioning brow as he took his usual place.

"I have to do it for Bella," Bishop explained. Archer nodded knowingly. Only a goalie would understand the need send mojo to a goalie that was hundreds of miles way. Bishop caught Archer repeating the motion before he had his usual talk with the goal posts. A few of the guys looked on curiously. Archer never strayed from his usual routine and to see that he would do that for Bella made him want to make sure they won this one.

He fell back into line as Preacher skated by him with the puck at his blade preparing for his shot. Bishop reached out and poked the puck out of Preacher's control and laughed at the glare he got in return. He stood just on the Warhorse side of the center line. He collected stray pucks until he had enough of them to snipe them at Preacher and Trevor's skates. It served to amp them up and at the same time the laughter let Bishop get rid of some of the tension he always carried during warm-ups.

As soon as they took their positions for the face-off Bishop immersed himself entirely into the first twenty minutes of the game. While DC had speed on their side, the Warhorses had a defense that was on fire. No one was getting close enough to the goal make a decent shot. Every person on the team made sure they were in the way, knocking the puck loose and pushing towards the other end of the ice in search of the first point.

Archer was proving invaluable when the defense couldn't get there. He gave everything he had and more to make sure they didn't hear the screech of DC's goal horn reverberate around the arena. Neither team managed to put up a point by the time the third period started and the frustration was starting to become palpable.

DC was starting to take cheap shots and Bishop was fighting the urge to be just as careless. He wanted to shove his stick against the back Daenville's shoulders and knock him teeth first into the ice for the way he shoved at Archer as he tried to flip the puck over his pads. Instead, Bishop bit his mouth guard hard between his teeth and swallowed down that fury and channeled it into making a play that they would succeed on.

All they needed was room for one pass, one block, anything that would allow Trevor or Morry a way to land the puck at the back of the net. The opportunity didn't happen until Andy took a stick to the cheek and they were on a power play. If they could keep the puck moving from player to player, it was enough to keep DC moving and trying to figure out what play the Warhorses intended to make. The puck hit the blade of his stick hard and he sent it on its way to Preacher and then to Morry and it was a sharp shot to get it across the front of the net and to Morry. Once Morry had control of the puck he turned it into gold. The lights behind the goal flared and Morry threw his hands up in celebration. Bishop crashed into Morry for a hug. It was a beauty of a shot and it took all of them to make an opportunity like that possible.

It was the best way to end a game. It was a stunner of a shot, and an upset for the home team and a win that would take the Warhorses into the next games. It was a rough schedule playing against DC, who was at the top of the division, always set them on edge. Winning against DC? That was the boost they needed to help them when the next few games. They were going to be depending on those points to push them into a playoff spot.

But first, Bishop's focus shifted from hockey to Barrett. He shifted in his seat to get comfortable for the next hour and a half. It had only been a few days but he missed the way Barrett always managed to touch him, even in passing. There was a selfish part of him that hoped Barrett would still be awake by the time he made it home.

He tried to keep his mind off of Barrett and what it would feel like coming home to him. He put his ear buds in and tried finish the last few chapters of his e-book. He couldn't focus on the words in front of him. All he could think about was being able to show Barrett how much he was truly missed him over the past few days.

As soon as they landed, Bishop grabbed his carry on and did everything he could to get away from chatty teams mates and out to his truck. He tossed his bag on to the floorboard and didn't waste any time getting away from the airport and on the interstate heading home.

The kitchen light was on in Barrett's house when Bishop parked in his driveway. He waited a few seconds before his phone vibrated in his pocket. He shifted and saw that it was Barrett.

"Don't tell me I stayed up for nothing?"

Bishop didn't even bother with his bag as he got out of the truck. He could deal with that in the morning. He had something better to think about. The front door opened as he stepped on the porch and Bishop's smile shifted from excited to predatory. Bishop was standing in the door way in sweat pants, without a shirt and his feet bare. His blond hair was ruffled and he wasn't wearing his glasses. Damn.

"Hey." Bishop whispered. He wasn't sure who reach out first but all that mattered was that his lips were pressed against Barrett's and their bodies flush against each other. The echo of the door slamming was forgotten in the frenzy of Barrett pulling the buttons of Bishop's shirt free as they shuffled towards the stairs. Barrett's hands were hot against his waist. His fingers dug into muscle to pull Bishop closer.

They stumbled up the stairs, dropping pieces of Bishop's game-day suit until Barrett smirked and whispered, "Pick that up. What if one of the girls wake up?"

Bishop hid his face in Barrett's shoulder to stop himself from bursting with laughter. His shoulders were shaking as he reached down to pick up the wrinkled clothing and made quick progress to Barrett's room. Bishop could feel Barrett's full attention on him as soon as they had the door closed and locked it. Barrett's fingertips brushed across every bump of muscle and skated lightly across the lingering bruises from hits that had been taken on the ice. Bishop swallowed down his need to rush past this, to take the focus off of him and put it entirely on Barrett. He let Barrett take his time. Tracks of heat were left by fingertips and had Bishop shivering with want.

Barrett wrapped his hand around the back of Bishop's neck and he searched out every reaction he had pulled from Bishop's body. Bishop's eyes dilated under the attention and his chest rose and fell with quick breaths. Bishop couldn't wait any longer. He leaned down, his lips caught Barrett's. He felt himself melt as Barrett slowly took control and his hands brushed along the small of Bishop's back. He let his fingers dip tauntingly into Bishop's pants. Barrett needed no direction. He started to work Bishop's pants open while his lips trailed down Bishop's jaw. Barrett stopped at the base of Bishop's throat. He let his teeth scrape at the tender skin. He alternated between soft soothing kisses and biting ones that made Bishop's fingers curl into his hair and he would tug, trying to get Barrett's lips on his.

His lips dropped open around a gasp from the first brush of Barrett's hand against his cock He needed more than these teasing touches and kisses that weren't nearly satisfying enough for him. He nudged Barrett back to get him on the bed. Bishop peeled his suit pants off and stepped out of them. He raised a brow at Barrett who was lounging on the bed watching him strip out of his shorts and socks. "Are you just going to watch or do you plan on getting out of those pants anytime soon?"

"What if I want you to take them off for me?" Barrett offered and Bishop didn't hesitate as he kneeled on the bed between Barrett's legs. He worked the elastic over Barrett's erection and took his time working Barrett's pants completely off. He wanted to drink in every ounce of Barrett's body. He looked long enough that Barrett wrapped his legs around Bishop's hips. "Stop looking and do something about it."

He didn't need any more prompting. He shifted forward, licking into Barrett's mouth as he rolled their hips together. He let the breathy moans that slipped from Barrett's lips guide him. He couldn't get enough of the man laid out before him. He wanted to taste every inch of skin and learn what made his body shake with need. He had ever intention in doing so until Barrett's hand, holding a condom bumped against his shoulder. Bishop glanced up and saw Barrett looking down at him, "Please."

The soft plea made his breath catch. The look in Barrett's eyes, open and completely trusting Bishop to take care of him. He struggled opening the lube for a moment before popping the cap open. Barrett shifted up on his elbows to watch as Bishop spread the lube over his fingers and raised a brow asking if Barrett was ready. He drizzled more over Barrett's hole before working him open. Once Barrett's body accepted the first finger, he worked his second in. He scattered warm, open mouthed kisses across Barrett's abdomen. He felt Barrett's fingers tangle in his hair urging him further down. He gave a teasing lick to the crown of his dick as he slipped a third finger into Barrett. Barrett's hands left Bishop's hair and tangled in the sheets and his hips raised up off of the bed making Bishop's fingers go deeper. He let out a heavy groan when Bishop's fingers brushed against his prostate. A bolt of pleasure lanced along his spine as Bishop continued to hit just the right spot.

It was beginning to become too much and if Bishop didn't stop, they'd have to go for a sleepy round two rather than the explosive sex he had hoped tonight would end with. He tapped Bishop's shoulder, "You stop that and get to the main show or I'm the only one with a happy ending tonight."

Bishop laughed at Barrett despite the glare he got in return. There would be plenty of time for the kind of foreplay he preferred. Right now was about making Barrett feel good. Barrett rolled the condom down Bishop's length and nodded that he was ready. Bishop worked himself slowly into Barrett. He rocked his hips until he was entirely inside him. He didn't move until Barrett tapped his leg. It was easy to get lost in Barrett and making sure everything was right for him.

He felt Barrett's orgasm tear through him. He tightened his thighs around Bishop and threw his head back as he stroked himself off with every thrust of Bishop's hips. Bishop tipped over the edge soon after. He wanted to fall asleep curled around Barrett but with a lingering kiss, he got up from the bed and walking into the bathroom to dispose of the condom and to wet a washcloth to clean the spunk from Barrett's skin. He made quick work of it and settled back in the bed behind Barrett and holding him close.

This was what he had been missing for so long. A partner, and someone who was just as concerned about him as he was them. How had he gotten this lucky? Barrett understood how important his daughter was to him, what hockey meant to him and how to support him through it all. Bishop tried his best to do the same for Barrett and hoped that he did. He wanted Barrett to know how amazing he was every morning he woke up and every night when he fell asleep. For however long Barrett would have him, Bishop would do his best to make sure Barrett knew how much Bishop cherished their time together.

CHAPTER 20

The last time Bishop had felt this happy with another person was when he had been a teenager at the boarding school. There was something exciting about experiencing all his firsts away from home and without the judgment of a small town following him around.

Now, Bishop couldn't imagine finding anyone superior to Barrett Griffin.

Barrett's arm was curled loosely around his waist and his nose tucked against the back of Bishop's neck. His entire body hummed with the satisfaction of last night. The thought of Barrett's lips hot against his skin and searching out all the spots that made his breath catch made Bishop ache with want. He wondered what Barrett would sound like, waking up to the sensation of Bishop's hands on his body and his lips tasting his skin.

He turned around in Barrett's hold intent on doing just that, but his bedroom door popped open.

"Dad! Miss Taryn got us pancakes! Ivy made a mess so she's helping her clean the syrup off of her. " Bella's voice made him jerk away from Barrett. He was wide awake and unsure of what to do. Part of him wanted to hide under the covers and pretend like none of this was happening. The other part, really wished he had at least a pair of boxers on.

"Bug? Can you go back down stairs and I'll be there in a few minutes. I need to hop in the shower and then you can tell me all about breakfast and the movie you went to see last night."

"Okay." Bella turned to leave the room and Bishop thought he was in the clear. Then it seemed to click in Bella's mind that Bishop wasn't alone and his bed partner looked a lot like their next door neighbor. "Why is Mr. Griffin in your bed?"

Bishop tilted his head up towards the ceiling and took a calming breath. "Give me a few minutes to get showered and ready for the day. Then we can talk. Okay?"

Bella narrowed her eyes. "Okay."

He rubbed his hands over his face in frustration. He glanced over towards Barrett who had been feigning sleep during the entire exchange. Now he had the bedsheets covering his head and he was laughing. Bishop shoved him hard. "You shit. You could have helped me out somehow."

"What could I say to that?" Barrett asked as he sat up. His blond hair was a wreck and there was beard burn on his neck and a few splotches on his chest.

"You were right there. There's no lying about that."

"Well, I guess it's time to let the girls know." Barrett shrugged.

"Fuck, I need a shower and clothes for this," Bishop grumbled. Barrett barked out a laugh and Bishop flipped him off before making his way into the bathroom. He poked his head out of the room after he turned the shower on. "She'll be back in here if we don't get done there fast enough."

"Why did we have girls? A boy wouldn't have noticed or cared enough to ask," Barrett mumbled to himself as he lay back in bed.

$

Bella and Ivy were both sitting in the living room with their arms folded across their chests. The twin looks of suspicion were too much for Bishop to handle without coffee. He slipped into the kitchen and Taryn had a cup ready for him.

"I'm so sorry. I didn't think she was going to take off running upstairs." Taryn sputtered out. "Bella was supposed to go get me another towel, not burst into your room like that."

He took a deep swallow of his coffee before reassuring her that it wasn't her fault. "It's fine. They were going to find out soon enough. She didn't see anything inappropriate."

"I'm still so embarrassed. We weren't supposed to come home for another hour, but Ivy was such a mess and I don't have a key to Mr. Griffin's house and heading back to my house would have taken half an hour. Plus we had already packed their stuff into my car. I didn't think anything like this would happen." Taryn kept going with her apology and it didn't look like she would be stopping anytime soon.

"It's okay. You take a coffee to-go. Recover. Then Bella and I will see you the day after tomorrow when I leave for the west coast games." Bishop patted her on the shoulder. He watched as she skipped making a cup of coffee in favor of grabbing her bag and making a hasty escape with one last apology.

"Is she okay?" Barrett asked as he padded into the kitchen rubbing a towel through his wet hair. He went straight for the coffee carafe to pour himself a cup. He took his first sip and raised a brow over the rim of his mug. "Are you ready for this?"

Bishop shrugged a shoulder. "Does Ivy not know about your preferences? Or is it shocking that it's the next door neighbor?"

"I think it'll be more of the, 'oh my god my dad is dating Bishop Briggs, hockey god!', that's how I think she'll react."

Bishop shook his head. "I'm not a hockey god. You know who is?"

"I don't even want to know. You'll just try to make me jealous." Barrett rolled his eyes. "Come on, we have children to scar and ruin their lives."

They took a seat across from the girls who looked like they were the ones in trouble. "Bella, do you remember or talk about knocking on my door if it's closed?"

"Maybe," Bella whispered.

"Well, this is your reminder, Bug." Bishop leaned forward and tapped her knee to get her to look up at him. "It's okay. I'm not mad."

"But why was Mr. Griffin in your bed?" Bella whined.

"What?" Ivy asked with confusion. She pinned Barrett with a look of confusion and suspicion. "Why were you sleeping with Mr. Briggs?"

"Mr. Griffin, Barrett, and I are..." Bishop trailed off and looked to Barrett. They hadn't expressly put terms to their relationship. It was awkward to use the word 'boyfriend' and 'partner' was a little too heavy. That was a term reserved for a relationship that had passed the year mark. At least, that's how Bishop felt about it.

"You know how Aunt Amelia brought Tommy to the cookout this summer at Mimi's house?" Barrett broke into the conversation. Ivy nodded in understanding. "Well, that's how Bishop and I are. We're dating like Aunt Amelia and Tommy."

"Oh, so you're boyfriends?" Ivy asked.

"Boyfriends?" Bella shrieked and it caused Bishop to grimace.

"Yes, boyfriends." Barrett answered. "That means I'll be spending more time with Bishop, just him and me. Then there will be times that we'll also spend time with Bishop and Bella together too."

"Okay." Ivy nodded.

"You're going to kiss too?" Bella scrunched her nose up.

Both Barrett and Bishop started laughing at her reaction. She was beyond disgusted with the idea that they would be kissing each other. It wasn't like Bishop was going to make out with Barrett in front of the girls.

"We still get to play hockey and go to games, right? Can we bring them to family night?" Bella started wiggling in her seat with excitement.

"Yes," Bishop nodded his head. "As long as that's what they want to do, they get to go to family skate night."

"It's the best night ever!" Bella said as she turned towards Ivy. She was off talking about what they did the last time. Bishop took that as his cue to make his way to the kitchen for a late breakfast. Barrett followed after him. "Does this mean we're in the clear?"

"I'd say so." Bishop grinned. "What do you want for breakfast?"

§

They didn't get to spend enough time together to satisfy Bishop before he had to pack his bags to head off to the west coast. He'd be gone seven days. He was lucky enough that he had enough time to see Bella off to school before he needed to go. He rushed through getting everything packed into his truck. He could feel Barrett's eyes on him as he handed over Bishop's backpack. Bishop leaned back against the door he closed and looked his fill. FaceTime wasn't going to be enough.

Barrett moved to stand in front of Bishop. He stepped in close and tugged lightly at his tie. "We're all going to miss you."

"I'm going to miss everyone too. I'll be busy but I'm going to call when I can. It might be late when I call though. I can text beforehand to see if you're awake if you want. I don't want to bother you and I know you have pages you need to finish inking." The words rushed from Bishop's mouth and he couldn't stop himself from talking.

"I'm not going to disappear on you while you're gone." Barrett's eyes crinkled with amusement. "If you're busy, I'll survive without hearing from you. Just score a goal for all of us?"

Bishop wrapped a hand around Barrett's neck and pulled him into a kiss. He wasn't sure why Barrett asking him to score for them made his blood run hot, but he would find a way to do it. Especially if it led to getting more kisses like this.

"You have to go or you're going to be late," Barrett said between kisses. His fingers were curled in the belt loops of Bishop's slacks and neither of them was willing to move away from each other.

"I don't care. They won't leave without me," Bishop mumbled and it caused Barrett to start laughing and he took a step back. Bishop wanted to reel him back in and bruise Barrett's lips even further.

"Okay I'm going." Bishop tugged his vest and his pants into their rightful places. "Go home before I'm late."

"Bye, Bishop." Barrett laughed. He stood in the driveway as Bishop backed out. He gave him one final wave before crossing their yards to start on his own work for the day.

• 193 •

They got back from the western game series with several wins under their belt. The Warhorses were sitting high in the rankings, and all the work they had put in on the penalty kills was paying off. They had hit a rhythm and despite just getting home, Bishop was ready for their next few games and then the bye week was coming up.

It was late when he pulled into the driveway and instead of going straight inside, he sent off a quick text to Barrett. "You up?"

"I am now. Meet you at the door?"

Bishop didn't bother to text back. Instead he slipped out of the truck, careful not to slam the door and jogged across their yards. As soon as he made up to the front porch Barrett pulled the door open. The sight of him made Bishop stop short. Barrett's was only in a pair of sweat pants and his arms were crossed over his bare chest. He wouldn't be able to pull off looking that good after rolling out of bed. The disheveled blond hair made Bishop want to curl his fingers in it, to get him at just the right angle to lick into his mouth.

Barrett smiled up at him, "Are you just going to stare all night?"

Bishop slipped his fingertips into the waist band of Barrett's sweat and gave them a teasing tug. His grin turned sly when he didn't encounter the usual boxers.

"We're on my front porch," Barrett said as Bishop stepped in until he and Barrett were pressed together, from thighs to hips.

"At least you don't have a babysitter to hide from," Bishop pointed out with a slight hitch of his hips. He wanted nothing more to push Barrett back inside and spend the night familiarizing himself with the taste of Barrett's skin again. He didn't give Barrett any time to respond. Instead he let a hand brush against the stubble of Barrett's jaw before dragging his fingers to the back of Barrett's neck. The kiss was slow as he reacquainted himself with what made Barrett's breath catch and how a subtle tilt of his head would always result in Barrett's grip tightening and his body pressing closer.

"I missed you," Barrett whispered as he pressed their foreheads together.

"I missed you," Bishop echoed. He had only been gone for nine days, but it felt like weeks. Phone calls, text messages and FaceTime could only do so much. Nothing compared to being able to to touch Barrett. They stood breathing each other in. They became a heady mix of spice and amber as they fell back into each other. Bishop didn't think he'd ever get tired of the taste of Barrett on his lips.

Being with each other like this, even a standing on Barrett's front porch wrapped together and stealing a moment of time, it was what Bishop had always wanted. The fact that Barrett was just as lost in this as he was, it made him want it even more. He pulled back reluctantly and pressed his lips together. "I'll see you in the morning?"

"Yes." Barrett nodded against Bishop's temple.

"Good." Bishop slipped in for one last kiss as a soft goodnight and he made his way across the yards. His heart stuttered in his chest when he looked back to see that Barrett was watching his progress. Everything in him wanted to jog back over to Barrett and spend the night with him, but he couldn't. Taryn was waiting to go home and Bella was expecting to wake up and have him be there in the morning for her.

One day he'd be able to go come home to the man he loved, his kids and be able to wake up next to man he loved. Until then, there'd be babysitters, late night visits, and dates to tide him over.

$

Bishop was barely awake when he heard Bella's alarm go off down the hall. It was only a few minutes later that Bella launched herself bodily onto his bed with an excited yell, "Dad! You're home."

"I am." Bishop rubbed the sleep from his eyes. "And I need a hug. I missed you."

Bella laughed as he scooped her up in a tight hug. She curled up on the bed next to him, "I missed you a lot."

"I'm sorry, Bug."

"You missed my second game," she whispered. "We lost."

"I know, but you know what happens when you lose against another team?"

"What?"

"You learn from it and become better. You might have missed blocking a shot, but now you know what you need to work on at practice. You know what to look for while you're on the ice and how to prepare for shots like that whenever you face it again." Bishop looked over at her to see her mulling his words over. Once she had settled on them, she nodded and reached out with her fist to bump knuckles with her dad.

"And do you know what?"

"What?"

"Family skate night is tomorrow evening. Maybe you can talk to Archer and get some tips from him." Bishop laughed at her excited wiggle. He had been keeping quiet on when exactly it was. He knew how much she was looking forward to going and he wanted to surprise her with it. He also knew that Barrett and Ivy were going to be coming as his guests. He was looking forward to being able to bring them to the rink.

The overly romantic part of him wanted to see if he could manage a date night, just he and Barrett at a rink, skating and having a make shift picnic. He wasn't sure if he'd be able to manage it, but it was something he might have to save for later and for something special.

"Can I skip school today? I missed you so much."

Bishop laughed. "No. You're already pushing. Go and get dressed. It's time to get a quick breakfast and get to the bus stop. I've got to go the grocery store and run a few errands."

"We can both skip?" Bella offered with the biggest smiled she could manage in hopes that he would agree.

"Nope." Bishop shook his head. "You're not sick and that means you're going to school."

"Fine. I still miss you, even though you're home," Bella grumbled as she rolled off of the bed and got to her feet.

"Way to guilt trip me, Bug." Bishop laid back and stared at the ceiling for a few moments before getting it in gear and getting ready. If he didn't beat Bella down stairs and have something figured out for breakfast he'd get one of those looks for giving up and just having her eat a peanut butter and jelly sandwich for breakfast and calling it good.

He got lucky when he found a box of cereal bars he knew Bella loved. They hurried out the door just when they heard the squeal of the bus's breaks at the stop sign a street over. He ignored the curious look he got from Barrett as he rushed Bella onto the bus. He turned towards Barrett with an embarrassed smile. "Good morning."

"Are you doing okay?" Barrett asked.

"I'm just tired and have a few things to do. Really want to go back to bed and just sleep until Bella comes home," Bishop admitted.

"How about you do whatever it is you need to do and I'll have an early lunch ready for us. Then you can nap until the girls get back from school?" Barrett offered.

"How are you so," Bishop fumbled with his words before settling with, "you?"

Barrett shrugged a shoulder, "It's nothing special and I don't have any work to do right now. I'm waiting for approval and feedback. Next week I might not be so nice."

Bishop chuckled softly as he reached out to press a kiss to Barrett's forehead. "Fuck it, I can afford take-out. I'd rather stay with you right now."

The satisfied smile he got from Barrett had him grinning just as widely. He let Barrett tangle their fingers together and lead him inside. They side stepped Ivy's hockey gear and her shoes that were piled up at the front door and Barrett led him wordlessly to his bedroom. It was warm enough in Barrett's room that he pulled his sweater off and tossed it at the foot of the bed before he crawled under the covers. Barrett tugged Bishop against his chest. Bishop's cheek pressed against his heart and his arm slid over Barrett's waist.

"Are you excited about tomorrow?" Bishop's voice was soft as he spoke. He didn't want to disturb the quiet of the room.

"That depends," Barrett answered.

"It depends on what?" Bishop tilted his head back to see Barrett better.

"Are we going as neighbors or are we going as Barrett and Bishop?" Barrett asked as he reached down to slip his fingers along the top of Bishop's hand. He traced the bones and veins, making slow patterns until Bishop shifted his hand enough to tangle their fingers together.

"I think we're going to go as Bishop and Barrett," Bishop said with a cheeky smile.

Barrett rolled his eyes. "So if I wanted to skate with you, hug you, and kiss you in the middle of the rink, would that be okay?"

"That would be perfectly fine." Bishop pushed up to lean over Barrett, his hands planted on either side of his head. He gently pressed his lips to Barrett's. He only lingered a moment before curling back into Barrett's body.

"It won't cause a scandal and get you in trouble?"

"I think it would cause a scandal if we didn't do any of those things." Bishop chuckled before admitting to how much he talked about Barrett to his team. "I might not have been able to help myself, talking about you. Don't be surprised if they know you and Ivy as well as they know me and Bella."

"You are the biggest dork." Barrett threw and arm over his eyes and his cheeks were flushed red.

"You like it." Bishop pressed a kiss to Barrett's chest and then his jaw popped with the force of his yawn.

"I will neither confirm nor deny that. Go to sleep." Barrett rubbed Bishop's shoulder. "We've got plenty of time before the girls get home."

$

Bishop woke up the sensation of Barrett trailing warm kisses down his chest and stomach. The scruff on his chin scratched against his skin and it little shivers of delight down Bishop's spine. He shifted to lie fully on his back and let his legs fall open. Barrett sank into the cradle of Bishop's legs with his elbows resting on either side of Bishop's hips.

"You're awake," Barrett said in between kisses. Bishop couldn't resist reaching down to slip his fingers into Barrett's hair. He tugged a little and Barrett hummed under his breath in approval. He tugged at the elastic waistband of Bishop's sweats and boxer-briefs. Bishop lifted his hips to let Barrett pull them down his thighs.

"This is the best dream ever." Bishop whispered.

"Not a dream," Barrett pointed out as he licked the underside of Bishop's cock. Bishop's fingers curled tighter into Barrett's hair. He moaned as Barrett swallowed him down with a soft hum. He had to focus not to let his hips roll up into the wet heat of Barrett's mouth. Barrett's head bobbed up and down on his dick. Bishop bit his lower lip and his muscles jumped when Barrett slid a hand up along his stomach and scratched blunt nails against flushed skin.

Bishop surrendered completely to each and every touch Barrett bestowed upon him. Fingers wrapped around him while one hand gripped his hips tight. Barrett's fingers left imprints and memories in their wake. His other hand teasing every dip of muscle he could touch. Bishop could feel the way Barrett's hips rutted against the bed top. He was so close, and all Bishop wanted was for Barrett come with him. He reached down, shifting his body until Barrett got the message and crawled up to meet him in a messy kiss. It was full of lips barely touching, tongues curling together and gasps when they finally gripped each other and worked each other to orgasm.

"You," Bishop started and instead of bothering to find the rest of the words he rolled on to his side and wrapped a hand around the back of Barrett's neck. He pulled him in for a slow, lingering kiss. "Please tell me we have time for a shower before the girls get here?"

"If we share," Barrett smirked. He rolled off the bed and finished the job of tugging Bishop's sweats off. "Come on, clean up. We've got plans tonight. I'm looking forward to skating with you."

There was something about Barrett saying that that made Bishop shiver as he pulled his shirt over his head and chased after him. Tonight couldn't come soon enough.

$

They were some of the last ones to the arena. Bella demanded to bring all of her gear with her instead of just her skates and helmet. That in turn, made Ivy want to bring everything because what if they decided to play hockey. They couldn't without their gear. That's what the coaches and their dads had always told them. No hockey without the proper gear. Bishop couldn't argue with that logic otherwise they'd try to pull the no gear line during the summer when they practiced on concrete.

"You're such a softie," Barrett whispered as they trailed behind the girls. Bella and Ivy could finally handle their gear like pros now.

"If I told them no, you know they'll try to use this as an excuse as to why they don't need their gear while they play street hockey," Bishop pointed out. "I'm not going to be dealing with broken bones, concussions and cut up skin until they're teenagers."

Barrett laughed. "Yeah. They'll bring their gear and not use it. I bet that's what you did."

"No comment." Bishop smiled as he led them over to where the majority of everyone was gathered. He got the girls attention and they went through the motions of saying hello, introducing Barrett to everyone's family and picked at a spread of food as they made progress through the group.

"Barrett!" Trevor Liou grinned wide when he spotted them and ran over.

"I'm his team mate and I've known him longer but he's more excited to see you." Bishop rolled his eyes and nudged Barrett off towards Trevor. "Go. I see Bella is already trying to put on her gear and it looks like she may be talking Archer into something in the process."

"You're sure?" Barrett asked.

"Go, mingle and meet the rest of the group. I'm sure you can commiserate with the some of the WAGs about my shitty habits." Bishop turned to go but Barrett grabbed his hand to stop him. He pulled Bishop against his chest for a quick kiss. "I promise you there will be no commiserating."

There was a loud cheer from Morry that caused Bishop to blush, "Go before I decide to give them more of a show."

Barrett laughed as he made his way over to where Trevor was finishing the introductions. Bishop watched just long enough to see Barrett shaking hands and exchanging a hug with Andy's wife. He walked over to where Archer was crouched down in front of Bella pulling her laces beneath her skate.

"Layer the laces," Archer explained and tugged them tight. "It adds stability. You can't just half-way handle your gear. This is what saves you from injury and you need to do it the best you can every time you put on your pads."

He watched as Bella unlaced and repeated what Archer had showed her. "Like that?"

"Exactly!" Archer held up a hand for a high five and Bella enthusiastically returned.

"Will you show me your stretches?" Bella asked. "I can't get all of my stretches all the way. I can't move around like the rest of the team."

"You will." Archer nodded. "You have to keep at it. When I first started I had trouble too. I'd put my gear on at home every day and would go through my stretches. We had a rink down the road from where I lived so I'd always be there practicing on the ice. But if you can't, then practice your stretches in the living room and while you're studying."

"Oh," Bishop groaned dramatically. "I'll never get her out of her gear now."

Archer chuckled, "You're going to have your hands full, that's for sure."

"Okay," Bishop reached down to help Bella to her feet. "Let me get my skates and you and Ivy put your helmets on and we can hit the ice. Only if you promise to go and eat some food when Barrett and I say it's time."

"Okay," both of the girls promised. He was quick to get his skates and to set out a pair for Barrett for whenever he was ready to join them.

Ivy's eyes were wide as they stepped on the ice. "I've got to be dreaming."

"Why do you say that?" Bishop asked as he skated backwards watching the girls step out.

"Because I'm skating here!" Ivy gestured around the rink. She pointed to the logo at center ice. "I get to skate where Warhorses skate."

"Well once you skate here you're an honorary War-horse," Bishop told her and he got an excited squeal from Ivy. Bella giggled at her before picking up a little speed. Ivy chased after her with a loud whoop. Bishop skated the length of the rink a few times before coming to a stop where a group had gathered. Barrett was laughing at something Preacher had said when he caught sight of Bishop watching him and slipped through the group to lean on the boards. "How did I know that they would get you out here before you could manage to do anything else?"

"Because I'm too nice."

"Well," Barrett grinned, "I think it's time I got to skate with you."

"I agree, because I still haven't seen you skate. I don't even know if you can," Bishop teased.

"Oh, I might be a little wobbly but I can manage."

"Good, your skates are waiting for you," Bishop leaned over the boards to look where he left them and pointed them out, "right there."

"You promise not to laugh if I bust my ass?" Barrett asked as he went to grab the skates. He stole one of the folded chairs to get them laced up.

"No laughing, I promise." Bishop glanced over his shoulder to check on the girls. He was not surprised to see that Archer had made it on to the ice with half of his gear on and was leading Bella through a modified version of his stretch routine. Preacher was passing a puck back and forth with Ivy.

"The girls are even occupied so you don't have to worry about them seeing you get hurt." Bishop smirked at Barrett who didn't even bother acknowledging the comment as he stood up. He pulled a toque out of his jacket pocket and pulled it on. The blond curls sticking out added with the black rimmed glasses were cute enough that he wanted to pull him into another kiss, but he would save that for later. He had plans to get that kiss later.

Barrett was a bit unsteady on his skates at first. He hugged the boards for a minute and then he reached out to grab Bishop's hand. "If I fall I'm taking you down with me."

"You're not going to fall," Bishop reassured him as they slowly skated. It felt like everyone was watching them. With a quick look over his shoulder, he saw most of the wives and girlfriends were watching them. A few of the guys gave them a considering look, but they went back to what they were doing, eating off of plates they brought in from the players lounge.

"Are you worried they're watching us?" Barrett asked.

"I'm more nervous than anything. I want them to lo—" Bishop cut himself self off. "I want them to like you ask much as Bella and I do."

"I've never felt more accepting into a group of jocks, than I have here." Barrett squeezed Bishop's hand.

"Good." Bishop bumped his shoulder against Barrett's. They skated slowly around to watch the girls. Bella was watching Archer intently, doing her best to imitate the exercises Archer was guiding her through. Ivy was playing keep away with Preacher and a Andy's boys. It looked like she was having way too fun being able to hold on to the puck as long as she was. Her tiny cackle made Bishop laugh. It didn't take long before Bishop was handed two of his own sticks. He passed on to Barrett who immediately tried to push it back into Bishop's hands. "I have no clue how to even hold that properly."

Preacher smirked as he skated by. "I'm sure Bishop will tell you just how to hold his stick."

Barrett's mouth dropped open in shock. His reaction was automatic. He reached out with the hockey stick and sent Preacher sprawling dramatically on the ice. It wasn't until he could Barrett's shocked look that he burst out laughing.

"Oh my god. I'm so sorry. I didn't even think, I just reacted and then you were falling. Are you okay?" The words spilled from Barrett's lips fast enough that it was hard to keep up with what he was saying.

"Dude," Preacher growled out as he stood up and dusted the ice from the seat of his pants. "You don't apologize when you pull a penalty. You own it, you sneaky fucker. I can't believe you got me."

Preacher wrapped an arm around Barrett's neck and tugged him in to a hug. "I see why Bishop is obsessed with you. You're full of surprises. I approve."

That was all Preacher bothered saying before he skated back off chasing after the group of kids. Bishop scratched the back of his neck hoping that Barrett would ignore the fact Preacher said he was obsessed with him. He was awkward enough. He didn't need any help in that department.

"So I heard something interesting while you were doing whatever you were doing," Barrett said.

"I feel like I should be afraid of what you're about to tell me," Bishop said as he spun around. He was skating backwards, facing Barrett.

"You've never brought anyone to skate with you here," Barrett said as he reached out for Bishop's hand. "Why is that?"

Bishop let Barrett tug him close as he tried to figure out what he could say to that. It was true. Besides Bella, he never invited anyone to any rink events. This was his space and he didn't trust or want to share this with anyone else. Not until Barrett.

They came to a slow stop. Barrett braced his hands on Bishop's shoulders to stay balanced as he waited for Bishop to talk. Bishop focused on the red logo under their blades. He didn't look up until he felt Barrett's cool fingers brush along his jaw and urging him to look up. "You're the only person I've ever wanted to bring here besides Bella or my family."

"I'm going to take that as the massive compliment that is and not look into it any further." Barrett slid his arm around Bishops neck, pulling him in close. He nuzzled his nose against Bishop's, teasing him until he couldn't resist any longer. His lips were cool against Bishop's. It was a subtle, lingering taste. It left Bishop's blood simmering from the attention and if they were alone he would have pushed for more. He pulled back to see how bright Barrett's gray eyes had grown under the lights of the rink. "You are amazing."

Barrett's smiled softly. "You're pretty great yourself."

"Well," Preacher yelled across the ice, "did he say yes?"

"I'm going to fucking kill him." Bishop pressed his forehead to Barrett's shoulder. He was shaking with laughter. "Can we pretend you didn't hear him?"

"It's Preacher, don't we ignore him anyway?" Barrett said as he wrapped Bishop up in a hug. "It looks like the girls have talked everyone into a game."

Bishop turned to look over his shoulder and pressed his lips together to stop himself from laughing. Both Ivy and Bella were standing, watching them with their arms crossed. Bishop could feel the force of Bella's eye roll from here. "We're coming. I'm on Ivy's team though."

"But," Bella started to protest but stopped, "Fine, Mr. Griffin is on mine. No trades."

Barrett shrugged a shoulder before knocking Bishop with his elbow, "I'm better than you."

"Yeah, right. You've never played hockey before." Ivy ratted her dad out without hesitation.

The mixture of families, significant others and professional players who took it too seriously made it easy to have fun. Barrett played just as dirty as Ivy did. She slid through Preacher's legs in attempt to steal the puck from Trevor. During a face off Bishop was set against Barrett. Barrett tried to distract him by attempting to kiss him. It didn't work. Bishop passed the puck behind him to Ivy. He laughed at the look of outrage that crossed Barrett's face as he skated past him.

After the game that Ivy swore they won two thousand to three, they demolished the remaining food in the players lounge. Bishop was pretty sure Bella had fallen asleep in her gear at the table. Ivy was listed to the side as she tried to tell Trevor a story about their latest practice, but she'd have to stop every few seconds to cover a yawn. They ended up carrying the girls out to Bishop's truck. They didn't even bother separating to their own houses. Instead the dropped the girls to sleep in Bella's room before doing the same in Bishop's room.

"Thank you for bringing us" Barrett said softly.

"There's no one I would have wanted to be there with us." Bishop mumbled into Barrett's shirt.

• CHAPTER 22 •

Bishop got home later than expected. It was three in the morning and all he wanted to do was fall into bed as soon as he got home. His shoulder ached from where he slid into the boards after a check knocked him off of his feet. He was surprised to see that Barrett's car was in his driveway instead of at his own house. He took that as a good sign. After the hellish loss they faced, it would be nice to curl up in bed with Barrett.

He took off his shoes at the door and padded through the house quietly in his socks. He stopped just shy of the kitchen. Standing upright on the counter was a book. He would recognize that artwork anywhere. No matter how tired he was, he wanted to see the finished result. He shed his suit jacket and his tie and then he grabbed the book. He stretched out across the couch and propped himself up with a pillow behind his shoulders. He reached to turn the table lamp on and thumbed open the cover. He was careful with the cover and made sure to take care of the spine of the book as he started flipping through the first pages.

He grinned at the tag-line of the book, "Huntington might not have much, but it did have hockey." No matter how tired he was, Bishop couldn't stop reading. He had to know what was happening to this ragtag bunch of hockey players trying to get on their feet and be the team they all knew they could be.

There were points that he wanted to reach out and touch the stitched on numbers and names on the back of the jerseys. He wanted to shake Benson, the captain, when he started to doubt himself. Then he wanted to cheer when the team pulled off a Hail Mary type of play to make it to playoffs.

He read every page and wanted more. He was a little too excited that there was going to be more to come. He wasn't ready to leave the Huntington Rams behind. There was more to their story. He had a feeling that Benson and Dominick might have had some romantic feelings for each other and if they didn't, he was going to be disappointed. He had become invested in a fictional relationship. How did that happen?

He read the author notes and finally the artist notes. Barrett gave a huge shout out to the Warhorses, but what surprised Bishop the most was what Barrett wrote about him.

'I'd like to thank Bishop Briggs. I don't think I would have gotten this right without his help. He let me talk his ear off. He answered every question I had and he never treated me differently for not knowing much about hockey. I can now say I'm fully immersed in the hockey culture and I don't ever want to leave.

Bishop, you showed me what a family is again. It isn't just your parents. It's the people who make you happiest. You, Bella and Ivy are my family. I don't know how you made it possible to look forward to getting up in the morning to stand at the bus stop with the girls, but you did.'

Bishop glanced at the clock in the kitchen and pressed his lips together. It didn't matter that it was barely five o'clock in the morning. He made his way to his bedroom with Barrett's graphic novel in hand. He sat on the edge of the bed and brushed his fingers through Barrett's hair. It only took a few passes before Barrett was nuzzling into the palm of his hand and waking up.

"Hey," Barrett whispered.

"I read your book." Bishop set it on the nightstand.

"How long have you been home?" Barrett asked.

"A little before three," Bishop answered. "I saw it on the counter and couldn't resist."

"What do you think?"

"It's amazing." Bishop leaned down to press his lips against Barrett's. "I read the artist notes."

"Oh?" Barrett's cheeks flushed.

"Yeah, oh." Bishop smiled at Barrett who was starting to look unsure of himself. Bishop wasn't going to have that. He didn't want Barrett to ever feel out of place or embarrassed. He stole another closed lipped kiss. "You know I love you, right?"

Barrett's sleepy smile made Bishop melt. Barrett plucked at Bishop's shirt. "Why are you still dressed?"

"I was distracted," Bishop shook his head fondly and let Barrett work his buttons loose. He tugged his undershirt free from his pants and fumbled with Bishop's belt.

"You're half awake and you're trying to get me naked." Bishop couldn't help but laugh.

"It's a rule. Someone says they love you, sex must happen," Barrett mumbled. He was slowly losing the fogginess of sleep as he got Bishop out of his shirt. He pushed Bishop down and let his hands trace over his abdomen and down along the cut of his hips. His thumbs pressed hard enough along the dip of muscle that had Bishop's lips parting around a moan. He shifted his hips trying to get Barrett to help him out of them, but Barrett's hand only tightened.

"But—" Bishop attempted to get Barrett to give some kind of response to his declaration but the warmth of

Barrett's mouth against his navel made him lose track of everything he was going to say.

"But,what?" Barrett asked as he straddled Bishop's thighs and worked his way up to Bishop's lips.

"I don't remember," Bishop whispered as Barrett licked at his bottom lip, biting just hard enough that had Bishop raising his hands to hold Barrett in place as he licked into his mouth. With every brush of his tongue against Barrett's, Bishop rolled his hips up against Barrett's.

"I want you," Barrett breathed out against Bishop's ear. He didn't need to say anything. Every move he made declared his intentions. It made Bishop yearn for Barrett. He arched against Barrett's hold and challenged him for control, even though he planned to give everything over to Barrett. His skin jumped under the light scratch of Barrett's nails across his skin. He became lost in Barrett's touches. Bishop could focus only fractions of a second before another touch ignited elsewhere on his skin.

He watched the muscles shift across Barrett's stomach, his chest and his arms as he reached into the bedside table. Bishop couldn't stop himself from reaching out to skim his hands along the sleep warm skin.

Barrett barely gave Bishop time to think as he dipped down, his mouth hot against Bishop's. Barrett tugged at the back of Bishop's thighs, lifting them higher and spreading him open. No matter how much skin he ran his hands, lips and tongue over, it still wasn't enough.

It was a rush, being able to trust Barrett enough to give him this much control. He hadn't wanted to share himself like this with another person until Barrett. He needed Barrett to know and never wanted Barrett to doubt how he felt about him. He lost his breath when Barrett started to work him open. It was on the edge of just enough to make Bishop's blood run hot. He'd never get tired of the way Barrett's hands grazed along the back of his thighs, along the back of his knees as he pressed soft kisses to tender skin.

Barrett moved slowly. Grey eyes focused entirely on Bishop and every breath he skipped, every gasp he made. Instead of two bodies trying to reach orgasm, they moved together to bring each other to the edge and then fell together. His body melted into the sheets and he couldn't keep his eyes open longer than a moment. He vaguely registered the touch of a warm cloth, wiping him clean. Barrett lay behind him with their knees tucked together. Their fingers tangled together under Bishop's chest. Laying with Barrett, he felt cherished and whole. He only hoped he made Barrett feel just as important.

Bishop slept through the alarm and through the girls getting ready for school. He probably would have not woken up if Barrett didn't urge him out of bed and into the shower. The girls would be getting off the bus soon enough and he needed to be somewhat awake when she and Ivy got home. "Bella just about murdered me this morning when I didn't let her come wake you up. It took a promise of making cupcakes with sprinkles after school to get her out the door and to the bus stop."

"You promised her what?" Bishop yawned.

"To make cupcakes when she and Ivy got home from school." Barrett repeated.

"You must really love my kid to promise her cupcakes. Bella and Ivy are going to be hell getting to bed tonight." Bishop started towards the bathroom to get showered and to try to be a functioning member of society for the remainder of the day. Barrett reached out and tugged Bishop into a loose hug.

"You know I do. Right? I didn't say it this morning, but I do. Love you. And Bella. I'd do anything for the two of you. You both make me and Ivy so happy. I thought that we would just be neighbors until you and Bella moved." Barrett slid his fingers in between Bishop's and brought their hands up to his lips. "You make me feel like I'm worth your attention."

"You are so much more than that." Bishop pulled Barrett into a tight hold. "You and Ivy, you're what I look forward to every morning."

Barrett started shaking in Bishop's hold. He took a step back to see that Barrett's cheeks were red and he was trying his hardest not to laugh, but it wasn't working out. "Are you laughing at me?"

"That was unbelievably corny. I can't believe I love you. You were waiting all this time to show me your true self. I feel in love with a jock and a dork. How is that remotely possible?" Barrett leaned forward to steal a kiss. And then another. And another. Bishop backed him against the counter, his lips curled into a smile and pressed against Barrett's. "You get to sit with the other significant others for every game you want to come to. And I get to know that you're there just for me."

"That turns you on far too much for me to even attempt to make fun of you." Barrett slid his hands up the back of Bishop's neck and into his hair. "But that's got to wait. Our kids are due to get off the bus."

"Our kids," Bishop grinned. "I like the sound of that."

"Let's go get them." Barrett reached out to tangle their fingers together. They sat on the front porch steps and waited for their girls to get home.

"Bella! Ivy! You're running out of time for breakfast." Bishop yelled from the foot of the stairs. He heard them darting back and forth from each other's rooms since Barrett woke them up for school. The only question was what were they doing to cause that much of a ruckus?

They had begun spending more and more time staying over at each other's houses, and after a long enough conversation they decided to put Bishop's house on the market and live in Barrett's house. The decision got them a lot of curious looks, but it was what made them happiest. Bishop couldn't imagine not waking up next to Barrett in the morning or having both Bella and Ivy screeching as loud as they could as they ran around the house.

"It's free dress day," Barrett pointed out as Bishop padded back into the kitchen. He was fixing Bishop his second cup of coffee for the morning while he waited for the toast to finish. "They've got plans and I'm sure we'll have to make them change before putting them on the bus."

"It'll be the first time Ivy isn't in Warhorse gear. You do realize this right?" Bishop asked as he put cereal, bowls, milk and spoons on the table. "Her teachers will call concerned about her wellbeing."

"I'll make you tell her teacher that we are now drowning in Warhorse gear because of you and need a break whenever we can get it."

"You love all my hockey shit." Bishop rolled his eyes.

"Sure do." Barrett smacked a kiss to his cheek and set his coffee down. "I'm going to go make sure our kids aren't plotting our demise."

"They're only seven and they have hockey practice coming up in a few weeks. They won't risk their only ride there," Bishop pointed out with a wry grin.

They both stopped talking as soon as they heard the sound of sneakers squeaking on the bottom stair like they did every morning. Ivy was the first one who walked into the kitchen. She was in her usual Warhorse tee-shirt with Bishop's name on and number on it. She had put on a white skirt, black leggings and her Chuck's. What surprised everyone was Bella. She was in a Warhorse Archer jersey and had the same skirt, leggings combination on as well.

They sat down at the table and started pouring cereal in their bowls. Bella felt both Bishop and Barrett watching her and looked up. "What?"

"Nothing, Bug." Bishop smiled into his coffee. "Looking good for free-dress. You too, Ivy."

"You have to put our bows in. Uncle Preacher gave us new ones for this season." Ivy slipped out of her seat and ran into the living room. She came back and handed them to Bishop. She turned around waiting for him to work his magic. He was better at fixing their hair than Barrett was. It made him laugh every time Barrett got fussy about the fact the girls always went to him to do their hair.

"There you go. I'll get Bella's when she's done eating. You two need to hurry up though or you're going to risk missing the bus and today I have plans."

"Like what?" Bella asked, before she shoveled a huge spoonful of cereal in her mouth.

"Like being lazy plans and they don't involve driving two little girls to school," Bishop explained.

"The best plans ever." Barrett commented with a happy sigh. He spotted the empty bowls and stood up. "To the bus stop. Your lunches are on the counter and your backpacks by the door."

"It's like you're ready to get rid of us." Ivy grumbled as she wound her way through the kitchen and towards the door. Both she and Bella shouldered their backpacks. "Bye, Dad Bye, Pops."

"Bye, Ivy, love you.!" Bishop yelled from the kitchen.

"What about me?" Bella whined.

"Bye, Bug. You know I love you."

"And if he doesn't I make up for it," Barrett added as he ushered them out the door. He stood by the window watching them until they climbed the stairs on the bus and headed for school.

Bishop slipped behind Barrett and wrapped his arms around his middle. He pressed a soft kiss to Barrett's neck. "You know what my favorite thing in the world is?"

"Is it Ivy?"

"She's part of it." Barrett smiled. "But it's more having all of you here. You, Ivy, Bella and me. I didn't ever think this would happen for us."

"You are so sappy sometimes, I can't handle it." Bishop teased before leaning in for a kiss.

"You love it." Barrett mumbled between kisses.

"Yeah, I really do," Bishop agreed.

With Thanks
In no particular order I promise

Crystal, it goes without saying that you will forever hold a spot in this section of every book I write. Without you, some of these ideas wouldn't have ever made it on to paper. You always encourage me to go for whatever it is that I want to write. Then you listen to me when I'm sure you get bored or tired of hearing about what I'm working on. I know you have a life that does not revolve around me. I'm beyond thankful that your family accepted me as part of the family. I still grin at being called Aunt Ashley. Purple is definitely the best color in the world. And how does Chris always know the right thing to say? Ya'll are and will always be my favorite gingers.

My Mom deserves all the love as well. Over the course of these past three books, she's showed me that I can be myself and embrace every aspect of that. I will always remember when Picking the Corners arrived while the extended family was over and she passed copies around for everyone to see, "hot of the press." That gave me courage I didn't think I had. Then there's the fact that everyone humors me at the house when hockey is on during family get togethers. Kimberly, Erika, Joey – I'm talking to ya'll. I know you don't watch hockey but a nine hour road trip with Kim, Erika and Joey listening to me ramble on about hockey games and players with a smile on their faces. Gavin, for a brother-in-law, you're awesome. , Thank you for giving me advice for my first signing. I've learned a lot from you over the past few years and hope to return the favor when I can.

Dad, I never thought I'd be able to share this with you but I'm glad you proved me wrong. While in Pittsburgh, knowing you talked about my writing and being there for a signing meant the world to me. I can't wait to show you what else I'm working on.

To all the readers over on AO3 as I mentioned in the dedication, if you wouldn't have cheered me on while I wrote fic, I don't know if I would have ever had the courage to put myself out there and to pursue my dream. I've met some amazing people. I've shared laughter and tears with you and I couldn't ask for better friends.
I consider myself extremely lucky for having each of you in my life.

ABOUT THE AUTHOR

Ashley K. Broome was born and raised in southern Louisiana. That didn't stop her from finding her love of hockey and embracing every aspect of it. When it isn't hockey season she's typically found sipping on PJ's Iced Coffee, nudging one of her three cats out of the way, or reading whatever book she can get her hands on. Playing the Point is her debut M/M Romance novel.

You can find Ashley K. Broome on Facebook:
https://www.facebook.com/authorashleykbroome/